GHOULISH BOOKS
San Antonio, Texas
www.GhoulishTales.com

Ghoulish Tales—Issue #4
Copyright © Ghoulish Books 2025
(Individual stories copyright by their respective authors)
All Rights Reserved

ISBN: 978-1-963801-06-4

PUBLISHERS:
Max Booth III & Lori Michelle Booth
EDITOR GHOUL: Max Booth III
LAYOUT DESIGN GHOUL: Lori Michelle Booth
ART GHOUL: Betty Rocksteady
ASSISTANT EDITOR GHOUL: Mindy Rose

CONNECT WITH US

www.linktr.ee/ghoulishbooks

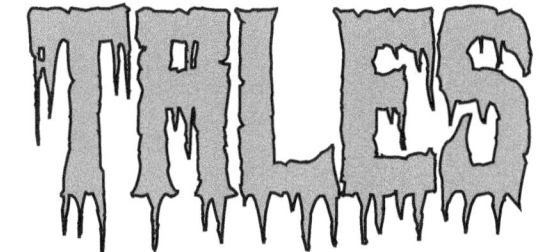

Issue #4

CONFESSIONS OF A HORROR POSER

HI, MY NAME IS MINDY, and I'm a horror poser.

Recently, my friend Max Booth (who you have probably never heard of, don't worry about it) shared a thought provoking essay they'd come across. Written by an esteemed colleague within the horror community, the essay detailed the stark differences between legitimate horror fans—worthy of calling themselves such—and people who claim the title but don't engage in true horror practices.

As I read through this essay, I was shocked and dismayed to find that I did not recognize myself among the ranks of those who truly desire to be disturbed; who wish to be psychologically damaged by each piece of horror media they consume, who don't even bother watching true crime documentaries unless they are promised each and every descriptive detail of the torture that was inflicted upon the victim. No, embarrassingly, as I went methodically through the checklist, I came to the shameful conclusion that I was firmly on the poser side of the spectrum.

It's difficult for me to admit this, but for the sake of transparency, it feels necessary: I don't enjoy things that make me feel bad. I don't enjoy things that upset me. I don't like reading about animals being abused, or watching profoundly brutal films. I like corny, predictable slashers. I like jump scares. God help me, I like *fun*. I like to have a nice, silly, moderately spooky time. I like gazing in gape-mouthed awe at icky, charmingly absurd practical effects.

As you can imagine, this revelation was quite jarring for me. If I'm being honest, it sparked a bit of an existential crisis. I started questioning whether I can genuinely call myself a fan of anything at all. For instance, I've unfortunately been aware for many years that I'm not a *real* fan of punk music, because I think the Sex Pistols sound like dogshit and Black Flag bore me to death. This harsh truth of course haunts me daily, and immediately came to mind as I began doubting myself as both a self-proclaimed lover of horror and, ultimately, a sincere human being.

Rather than continue on the dishonorable path of the poser, I've decided to start taking steps to desensitize myself so that I may become numb to—

Nah, I'm just fucking with you. Max *did* show me a post from some pissbaby edgelord whining about 'horror posers,' but can you imagine giving a shit? Lmao! We had a nice time making fun of that person, and then Max suggested I use that poser line as my intro to this thing they want me to write, so I did. They also suggested that I talk a bit about how I first got into horror, but truthfully, I don't fucking remember.

It would be super cool to be able to recount an experience during which small Mindy had snuck downstairs after bedtime and caught an episode of *The X-Files* that blew her tiny mind, or perhaps stumbled across a battered VHS of *Sleepaway Camp* in the gutter and was forever changed, but alas! Neither of those things happened.

(I did once stumble across a VHS in the street, but it was the 1994 action-romance film *Speed*, starring Keanu Reeves and Sandra Bullock [Great movie, highly recommend.].)

When I scour my mind for standout horror memories, by far what I've been most impacted by was reading *The Amityville Horror* when I was eleven years old. I picked it up solely because it was A Book That Was In My House, and no one stopped me from reading it because it was the 90s. That book, to put it lightly, severely fucked me up. I was just a dumb little kid, so the "Based on true events!" boast on the front cover could just as well have said "literally every single god damn thing written in this book actually, for real, happened." Long story short, I had a bizarre fear of both flies and pigs until I was fifteen.

So like, *that* happened, but that's more an anecdote about me . . . *hating* horror, which is not at all what Max asked for. I am failing this assignment!

Really, I was just always a Halloween Kid. I adored a bit of gentle spookiness, and I've viewed the world through a slightly distorted lens of creepiness for as long as I can remember—the leaf blowing across the road is always, first and foremost, a sinister skittering beastie, the power outage surely caused by a masked, axe-wielding intruder, the growl in the night is never my dog, but a demon in the walls. One of my toes is eternally edged just outside of the circle of salt, baiting a sweet, fleeting scare.

Despite this disgraceful preference for the more lighthearted side of horror, Max has allowed me to join their Ghoulish empire, first as Publicity Ghoul, then assistant slush reader, and now, tentatively, as an editor as well—my foray into which began as follows: I asked Max "Would you wanna, like, teach me how to edit, maybe, at some point?" and Max was like "Yeah, maybe, at some point," and the next thing that happened was that Max sent me the stories that are contained within this very issue of *Ghoulish Tales* and said, "Here, try to edit these."

So, reader, I tried. And here we are. I'm . . . an editor? While this is the first *Ghoulish Tales* issue to feature yours truly under the Assistant Editor role, we *also* did a fun thing with the submission process and only considered writers who had never been published

before, which means that this issue contains six stories from six authors who, at least at the time of their acceptance, had previously never published fiction. We are fiercely pleased to be the ones to grab them by the throats and fling them off the cliff of novice writers and into the churning and savage sea of published authors.

I could go on and on about how honored I am that Max trusted me enough to let me shove my grubby hands into this art and twist it up into new shapes, and I could make a lengthy list all of the big gross emotions I have about it, but no one wants to read that and more importantly I do not want to start crying while writing this right now, at 3:34am. So. Thanks. I hope I didn't fuck it up too badly.

—Mindy Rose
Assistant Editor
Ghoulish Tales

Subscribe to
THE GHOULISH TIMES

Keep yourself updated with everything going on in the world of GHOULISH by subscribing to our newsletter, The Ghoulish Times!

Essays, interviews, and even occasional fiction! Plus, photos of our cute dogs.

Everybody in your neighborhood is already subscribed.

WHY AREN'T YOU?

https://buttondown.email/ghoulish

CHEWINK CHEWINK

Miguel Villa

THEY DON'T TELL you the monsters you'll face when you're all alone.

They don't prepare you for those battles.

Have you ever tried putting an Icy Hot patch on your own back? It's impossible. They should put a warning on the box: you need at least one person who loves you, to put this patch on your back.

They don't tell you that one day, you will find yourself sitting in the driver's seat of your used 2017 Toyota RAV4 trying to figure out how to get this Icy Hot patch to stay on the seat so that you can re-stick it to your gross, slick back.

They don't tell you that while this is happening, a family, out walking their dog, will notice you, shirtless, sweating profusely, nipples perky and alert, grunting, mumbling to yourself, and they will slowly cross the street with their adorable child. The child will look over their shoulder and you will lock eyes, immediately recognizing the pity they hold. You will turn away before the pain becomes too much to bear.

They don't tell you that you will hurt your back while helping your cousins' live-in fuckboy carry an unnecessarily heavy cooler filled with beer and Kool-Aid jammers from one Mexican family party to the other.

They don't tell you that later that night you will almost piss yourself because you couldn't lift the toilet seat. No amount of yelling or crying could convince your body to just let you do this one thing. You will instead pee in the sink. It will not be the first time. It will not be the last. You will splash some water around the basin to clean it. Fucking Kool-Aid jammers.

They don't tell you that you need a new "In Case of Emergency" number for your cellphone.

Your fucked back reminds you that you are forty-two, overweight, average height, average intelligence, and desperately holding on to your hairline as vigorously as someone holding on to the edge of a cliff, staring down into the abyss below.

They don't tell you to protect your hairline. Why don't they tell you that? Why isn't that something you learn in high school?

They don't tell you that after peeing in the sink you will go to Walgreens to buy some pain meds. While there you will drop your keys on the ground while attempting to get out of your used 2017 Toyota RAV4 XLE with the upgraded roof rack. You will look down at the keys, next to a black spot you're pretty sure is the desiccated corpse of a grackle. The grackle corpse will wink a maggot-encrusted eye at you. You won't wink back. *CHEWINK CHEWINK.* Its song will take you back to that country road black top, back to the plague of grackles.

You will think . . . you can keep them, and walk into the Walgreens without the keys.

They don't tell you that the store brand pain meds are on the bottom shelf.

They don't tell you the visions will start on a Sunday drive, through the countryside. First one grackle corpse, and then another, until the road is black with their broken bodies. You pull over and listen to them for hours until a police cruiser finally shoos you away.

They don't tell you that your friends, no matter

how much they love you, can't always be there for you. They have their own lives. You can't ask your friend to leave their home, to abandon their anthropomorphized hedgehog video game, drive to the Walgreens and pick your keys up off the ground. How do you explain that without bringing up those goddamn Kool-Aid jammers again? And what if they don't see the grackles in the parking lot? What if they don't hear them, singing their little songs through putrified lungs? What happens then?

They don't tell you it will take twenty minutes for the 650 milligram TYLENOL® 8 HR Muscle Aches & Pain caplets to start working, that you will wait outside your car until the pain subsides enough to bend over and pick up the treacherous keys. They will fall out from between your nails the first time. You will exhale and try again. As you retrieve them, one of the grackle corpses will turn to you, worms writhing in its ripped-open chest— and you will swear, buried beneath its horrible grackle song, it starts talking to you. "This is where you belong," it will say. "This is where you've always belonged." You will remember this message from that Sunday, out in the country.

They don't tell you that when you think you've reached your lowest point, you have so much deeper to fall.

They don't tell you that as you enter your used 2017 Toyota RAV4 XLE with the upgraded roof rack and 96,000 miles on it that the bottle of pills will come loose from your grasp and fall to the ground, next to the grackle corpse, and slowly roll into its bloody, rotting embrace. You will cut your losses. You won't need those pills when you're on the ground, anyway.

They don't tell you that eight-hour pills don't really last eight hours. But they will last long enough for you to crawl into bed. You will look for your phone and spot it on the other side of the room, on the dresser. You will decide to masturbate the old-fashioned way, withdrawing ancient material from the spank bank. Ten unfruitful minutes later you will chance it and make for the phone, where a voicemail awaits you.

They don't tell you your ex will contact you at the worst times.

They don't tell you that you can no longer start stories with "my wife and I."

They don't tell you that nighttime is the loneliest. That it's when the monsters come out, when the voices get the loudest. The ones that say nobody will ever love you, that you're not worthy of love. That the love you need can't be given by a human.

But *they* can. The voices in the dark can love you. They can envelope you in their bloodied oily wings. "Come to us," they will sing, every night, until you finally muster the courage to listen to the voicemail. *CHEWINK CHEWINK,* the birds will scream in your ear. *CHEWINK CHEWINK.*

And the last thing you ever think will be, *Motherfucking Kool-Aid jammers*.

FLOWERS OF MY LONG DEAD GRANDFATHER

Harrison Stypula

YOU GOT TO know three things in life to keep yourself sane and not dead: where you've been, where you are, and where you're going. At least that's what Pappy always used to say. Get all those thoughts in order and you're going to be alright in the end. He believed that right up until Pollination started and he got taken out to pasture. Now, I just see him waving in the fields. His stalks have grown up to right about neck-height by now. Tall enough that if you hold your hand out in front of him, he'll high-five you in the blowing wind. Watching his stems fill out into buds at the beginning of every growing season always helps me keep track of the time. I know it does for a lot of other folks, too.

Pollination started not too far back, at least in comparison to how long history itself is. History books always confounded me, so I just stopped reading them. Pappy always had better stories to tell than they did anyway, or at least he told them better. Stories about where he'd been, and what he'd done, too. Some of those things he talked about I had to do eventually myself, though I didn't want to. But the hard things were much easier to do having heard him talk about them for hours at a time. Hearing those stories may have helped me do what needed to be done, but even so they still weren't even the most fantastic thing at home.

Music was always a mystery to me, with the way it made me feel better than anything else, even Pappy's stories. Singing and praising the livestock for good sustenance before they up and left was one thing, but the records Pappy brought home with his new machine were something else entirely. The music he put on that old gramophone was something you couldn't even imagine. It was the kind of sound that resonated through my very soul. Since he got that machine I swear I never heard a more heavenly melody in my life. Listening to it blasting out from the speaker while I worked what was left of the fields made me want to swing harder, hoe longer. Beat the ground senseless until I dug up some precious piece of soil that would grow the crops nice and tall to keep us fed for another season.

Not long after Pappy bought that gramophone, though, the soil stopped growing things all together. The earworms I got from the music were the only sort of worms we'd seen in a while, and that lack of worms had Pappy feeling more than anxious.

He'd inspect the soil for hours at a time, trying damned near as hard as he could with his aching back. He plunged two fingers into the dirt beneath the dry topsoil I had finished plowing and they returned to the light with little flecks of brown crust. He stuck his fingers in his mouth and sucked deeply, as if the taste would somehow answer all of our problems.

"I'm telling you now," he said, "I know right where we're headed if we don't fix things here. We're gonna be fucked if we don't bring the land back to us."

Like a foolish child, I turned to him and asked, "You really mean it, Pappy?"

"Does my face look like it's lying?"

He stumbled off back to the house, and I didn't

hear him speak again for the rest of the day. No stories that night. No music. The silence was enough to make me tear up a little bit. Even some crickets would have been nice to hear, but they disappeared just about the same time as the livestock and worms. Nothing left to hear now, not even a single chirp.

When we heard about Pollination from the folks a few farms over, it sounded like it was going to be the answer to all our problems. The first thing that crossed my mind was how confusing the name was, especially since our problems weren't with pollinating the crops at all but getting them to grow in the first place. Though this didn't matter for long; once the fellas in purple suits started prancing around the fields in their oversized galoshes, things seemed like they might finally be improving. I was certain that whatever fancy equipment they brought with them was going to make the fields prosper again, and in their own way I suppose they did.

Pappy got his pistol out the first time they showed up, ready to take a few good shots at the purple fellas invading the fields. He couldn't stand it when anyone trampled on his land when they were freshly tilled and planted. Even if it was one of the sheep that wandered out of the pasture and onto the land, he'd take a shot at them. Now, usually he'd miss, leaving it with some singed holes in its wool, but there had been a few that had flopped over onto the ground after the bang. Sometimes I used to wonder if it was all that blood he spilled there—that it angered some old, dead, sheep-god who cursed our lands, but now I don't know so much if I believe that. In fact, I don't know what to believe anymore. I didn't let him get any shots off, though. I imagined they knew what they were doing. Now, I suppose so did my Pappy. He probably saw what was coming, more or less.

It didn't take much longer than that for Pollination to begin in full. Paper flyers went up all over the town, from what we heard from the Peterson farm just over yonder, and even out this far the old telephone poles that held no purpose anymore were tacked with bright, canary yellow flyers that all had the same announcement: *Pollination Day. May 15th.* I didn't know quite what they meant, and neither did Pappy, but he seemed all shook up about it.

I didn't put up much fuss when the purple suits came to the house directly, and didn't just stick to wandering the fields. Since that first time when Pappy almost got some shots off at them, I had taken to keeping all the bullets out of his pistol, just in case. It was good, too, because that was the first thing he went for when they returned and clomped through the door without so much as a hello. They weren't violent, but smooth and quiet as the night air. Light purple specters who waltzed through our living room while Pappy yanked on the trigger of his pistol, clicking it in confusion at the lack of shots, before finally resorting to using it as a club like some sort of caveman. I cranked the volume on the record player to drown out the sound of them taking my Pappy outside to the fields.

Since the day before, when I'd watched the same thing happen on the Peterson farm, I had been expecting it here. Only, instead of behaving like Malcom Peterson, who tried fighting to protect his ma and pa, whose limp body fell to the ground after one of the purple suits shot him dead between the eyes and quickly hauled him out for Pollination alongside his parents, I stayed put. I didn't do anything to stop them.

Blasting the Requiem and sipping a glass of lukewarm tea, I stared through a dusty window as the purple suits took him out into the fallow and tied him up to what looked like a great, big bean pole. I thought it was a fitting piece to listen to, given how Pappy told me it meant something like "remembering the dead". While they tied him to the bean pole, I watched in wonder at the process they took to calling Pollination, though it wasn't anything like the sort of pollination I was familiar with. Using stakes shoved into the ground and ropes to hold him upright, they let him wiggle there like a worm, squirming against the restraints, until one of them finally stepped forward and stuck a needle in his neck that made him go limp. My Pappy always preached about the sacrifices you sometimes needed to make to keep the land providing, and I made mine, no matter how difficult it was.

Over the course of the next few days, I stayed inside and ate up most of our supplies, because I was too afraid to go outside where they left him. They came back almost every day I waited, checking him over like doctors would and giving him more of those needles to the neck and slipping long, metal tubes under his skin.

It wasn't until the plants started growing out of him that I realized they were doing what I had done for years in the fields, only with his skin and meat. It was then that I went outside and walked right up to him, staring at the ungodly sort of scarecrow Pappy had become, and at the little sprouts emerging from his skin. My curiosity made me want to poke at what was left of him, if only to see what it felt like. Just before I was able to make contact he writhed under the ropes, his eyelids flashing open to reveal the yellowed, wrinkled balls that were what was left of his eyes.

I fell back on my rear end and almost lost it then, but as he slipped back into whatever dream they put him in and I watched the little vines sprouting from his arms grow just a little bit longer, I realized there wasn't anyone left to help me keep track of myself. I knew that what was gone was gone and was never coming back. Where I was right then, sitting beneath the hulking thing Pappy had become during Pollination, I made the choice to cultivate these new plants just like I would any other crop, seeing as they were the first things that had grown on our land in the longest while. Things would be okay if I did that, and his sacrifice wouldn't have been all for nothing.

As I sit here now resting in the crops, looking about the field that's grown a hundred times the size it was before Pollination started, it's hard to believe it all started with just one plant.

It was a few months before Pappy *really* started growing. Once he stopped moving, I was worried the plants would die too, but they grew up quick, with plenty of vigor. By the time his meat had mostly withered away and he really looked like a scarecrow, just a frail skeleton with a paper-thin mask of skin, the fellas had brought over another pole and plant.

They plopped it down wordlessly into the soil beside Pappy and it took me ages to realize it was Pa Peterson. He was just another funny looking scarecrow, all skin and bones. By the time a year had passed, I had dozens of plants to take care of, thanks to the purple suits. Though they never said it, I feel like they wanted to reward me for being

such a good farmer. I've kept them healthy and flourishing multiple seasons now, and produced more crops than I can count. I *am* a good farmer.

Right now, I'm growing something sort of like corn, and I think Pappy likes it a lot. He doesn't grow as well as he used to. I think he might be all used up now, but I like keeping him around. Even without the crops he still grows some awfully nice flowers. I sit by him most days after work, the record player blaring from the house like it used to, loud enough that I can hear it out in the field next to him while his limp hands blow around in the breeze. But something else is on the breeze now, too.

Just like the flyers for Pollination got tacked up to start out, a few weeks back the purple suits started putting up new flyers talking about bringing back the livestock too. They even were nice enough to let me know they'd be coming today. Not directly of course, by the big, bold letter they tacked to my door was nice enough, in their own way. In fact, I think I see their truck coming up the way now. It's no matter, though, the drive is long enough before they get here that I got some time to finish writing up my thoughts here.

I couldn't be more pleased that they thought I've been doing such a good job with the people-plants that I'm well off enough to take on the honor of getting a few animals of my own. Raising some critters, though I don't know quite what kind yet, it's going to be so rewarding I just know it! They'll make for nice company, I'm sure.

You want to know the funniest thing, though? It's so odd but the noise those animals are making from the truck sounds almost human, but that's okay. If I can manage the people-plants, I can manage whatever newfangled animals they've brought me. I just took one of Pappy's flowers and stuck it behind my ear, thinking how nice I'll look for the new arrivals. Even after everything that's happened, I know just where I am, and I've never felt better about where I'm going.

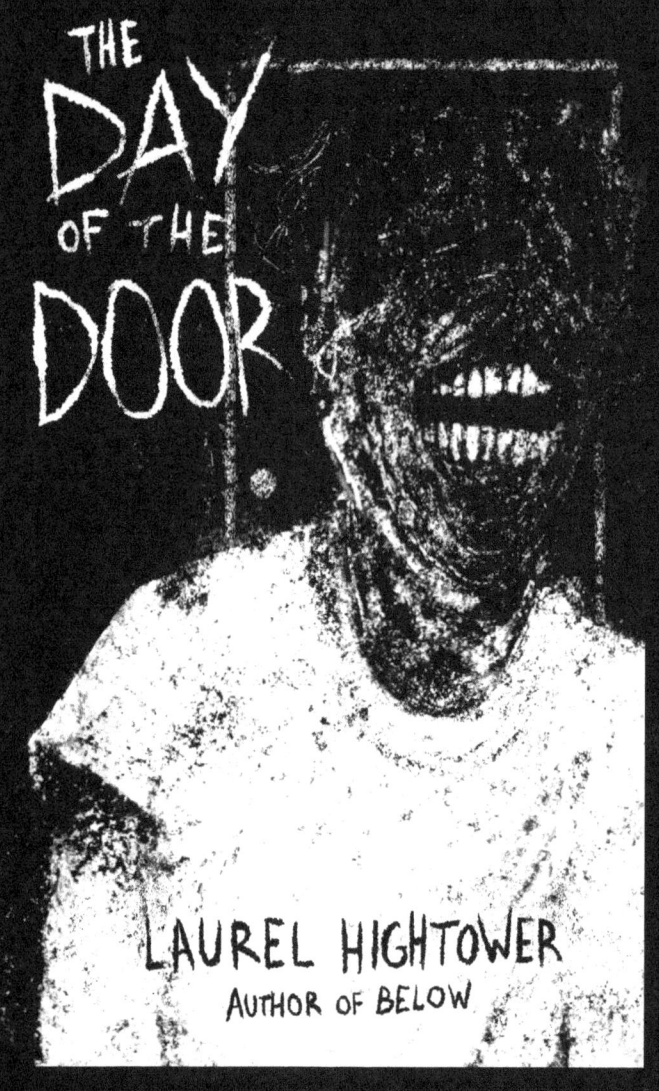

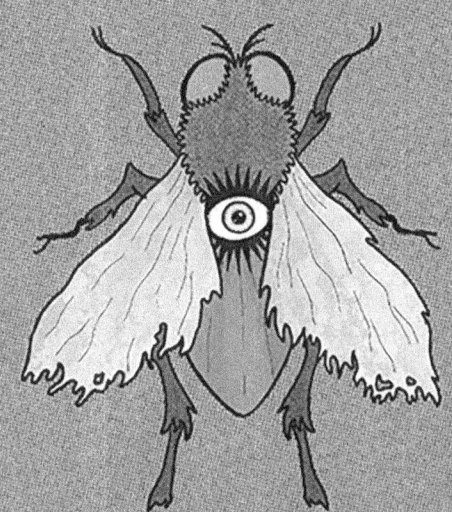

TOXICITY

MAX BOOTH III

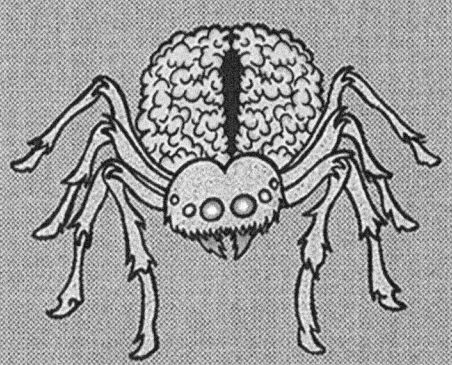

THE MIND IS A RAZORBLADE

MAX BOOTH III

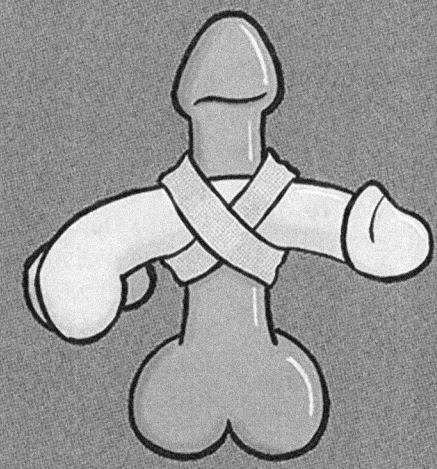

HOW TO SUCCESSFULLY KIDNAP STRANGERS

MAX BOOTH III

WWW.GHOULISH.RIP

XYLOPHONE BONES

M.M. Williams

TINK, TINK, TINK go the xylophone bones. You call them bones—they look like ribs. When the traveling musician came to the Blighted Borough on a charitable jaunt, he said nothing, only played, only gave the sickly children little xylophones, and now the filthy alleys sing.

To our north, the tall buildings of Inner Sternham block the sun, and to our south, the forest looms, but for once, the bloody shadows between—our native grounds—know music. We know music and even the thieves, even the rippers, even the gangs stop to listen.

She plays the bones, though she cannot see them, and you watch her. You watch and watch and cannot stop. *Such beauty*, you tell me on a sigh, *can't be real.* We invite her to our hidden nest in the west, our overturned fishing boat in the tangled trees on the riverbank. You introduce her to our dearest friends, the swallows and the sparrows. The more she plays, the more you sing, the more I dance. In these bones, we've found home.

On days when the chimneys are too tight and the climb scrapes my skin and crushes my bones, I dream of the moment when I will return and sleep as you play. On nights when wolves or men are prowling and we must sit back to back without a flame, she tells us the rumors of what lives across the river, in the inner city where the buildings stand tall and the clothes are clean and the children need not hide.

There, on those clean streets, in the parlors of the high houses, in the king's hall, they don't drink rain and eat grubs, or duck away from thirsty blades and snatching hands. They sing and play on more kinds of bones than we can imagine—pianos and strings and flutes. Some buildings exist only to house the music. Some people exist only to play it. How amazing and good and kind those souls must be, to be so blessed.

Perhaps that's why, along with the music, they have the food, the firewood, the smiles.

Winter arrives some months later, and it is bitter. Smoke rises from the high house chimneys, but not from the Blighted Borough. Carts arrive from the inner city and take from our storehouses, from our bakers and cooks, from our woodsmen and smiths. All that remains is blue, wormy bread, sodden with filth, unfit even for the swine.

Before long, we dare not enter the streets in the daytime. Blood spots the snow as the weak become the feast. We dare not leave the boat at night either—only fools chase the kiss of the midnight wind.

Our stomachs demand we search, but nothing swims below the glass surface of the river, nothing wriggles under the frozen bark of the trees, and only one choice remains for us. With a tear in your eye, you hold your hand to the sparrows. Brown feathers and tinkling whistles descend to your knuckle. The bird sits upon your finger, then in your palm, then curled in your fist, and as you weep, your teeth cut the sound in two.

Above a meager fire, on shards of old pots, we lay the meat, and what was once music turns now to sizzles and pops. That night, the bones stay quiet, and as we eat, we mourn.

When you sing next, however, the tone is more beautiful than before, and she calls it the bird's parting gift. Practical soul that I am, I know it to be the power of a full belly, but you—as you have always done—hold to a more lyrical theory; its song now lives in you.

Over the coming nights, we must do the same again, but your regret is less. Blood coats your lips like sacramental wine as you whisper pleas for their forgiveness, but you do not mourn. Instead, you practice. When the ice melts and spring blinks out of his slumber, you and her cross the bridge to the foot of the high houses, and your new song brings a copper into our hat.

Years pass by with a tink, tink, tink. No longer can you nor I fit in the chimneys, so we find ourselves instead in the factories, crafting wheels for the fine carriages across the river, fine plates for their tables, fine jewelry for their ears. In the nights, we cross the bridge and sing and dance. And as our bodies grow, so do our hungers. Along with food, we crave more songs, more bones, more birds.

We want to know the music that the high houses know.

Near the edge of our city of Sternham, some miles from the Blighted Borough, the circus visits. In tree branch thrones under a chandelier of stars, we watch distant shadows writhe on glowing red canvas. She is in your arms. Birds perch upon our toetips. A name reaches us, carried by a booming voice. The Starling. The Starling, the people's darling, is here. The crowd within stills and quiets. Even from here, we hear the clack of the heels, and from the ground rises a silhouette of generous hips and a grand wig.

And she sings, the most powerful bird we've ever known.

I cannot breathe—I almost wish not to, lest I take the air the Starling needs and her song should end. Up and down she travels, fast and slow. The flutter of a hummingbird's wings lives in her throat. It ascends like a mountain, then falls back into a gentle stream.

Much too soon, it ends. You cry, and she cries against your shoulder, and you share a smile and a kiss. I rub my gooseflesh back to skin.

As we're walking home, and you look over your shoulder at the tent, yet another new hunger enters your eyes, one I ask about.

What she has, you tell me, *can be mine.*

Evening after evening, you disappear, and we work, perform, and beg alone. When the moon is at its peak, you return. *Practice, practice, practice,* you mutter in your sleep, *soon to find perfection.* A week passes into memory, and when the circus wagons groan their way to places unknown, you return and nudge me out of sleep.

Listen.

Your lips part in quiet song, and in our rotted home, I hear the Starling once again. The voices, yours and hers, could have grown upon the same branch. Twin cherries, equally sweet. A voice worth a hundred coppers. How you've accomplished this so quickly, I do not know.

A price was paid.

I ask how much—we don't have anything to give, neither is there much to steal in this borough, and you would never place your neck in the jaws of the creditors.

I've done some harm.

To that, I have no response. From your pocket comes a necklace with three beads as azure as the evening sky, the beads you make in the factory. Had you been caught in your theft, your fingers would have been forfeit—no one steals from the men across the river. When it's fastened around her neck, you take your place at her sleeping side, your nose below her ear, your fingers resting in the ridges of her ribs.

Anything, you tell me, *to make her warm.*

It isn't long before our performances begin to make horsemen and carriages stop, and our hat fills enough that we can leave the boat behind. For the first time since our very first night, you and I know the wonder of a roof and door. The swallows and starlings follow you. One room is all we need, we three. With what we have left, she builds new bones, I find new shoes, and you sing louder than ever.

The former ringer of the church bells is buried, and the vicar knows of your song and her talent. He bids you work for him. Whatever lives above the Blighted Borough, we do not worship; nonetheless, you agree. The gangs, superstitious beings that they are, protect the churches. The churches protect their own. They will marry the two of you free of charge, and a small home near the old chapel will be yours.

So, you leave our room and take many pieces of me with you, but above all, I am happy. I work and gather alone in the days and sleep alone in the nights. When the bells go ring, ring, ring, I think of you and the dream in which you live. She learns the bones of the organ, and you learn to read the notes. Your voice quickly becomes legend in our borough and beyond, even worthy of invitations to the holy cathedrals across the bridge.

I visit each week. Some years go by before I'm invited to dance in a hall in the inner city, and I cannot resist the promise of dependable coppers and meals. I plan our farewell, for I know that your home is here and always will be.

But when I knock upon your door, you do not answer.

When I slide a knife through your window lock, I don't find you or her inside. When I sit in the church pews, no organ plays, and you do not sing. No swallows or starlings sit upon the clotheslines above the streets. Two weeks pass, and then I truly begin to fret. Where you've gone, I do not know, but terrible things are wont to happen in this Blighted Borough.

I search high and low. I ask others if they've seen you—the one beloved by birds, the one who looks like me—and none can answer. I ask them if they've seen her, the woman whose songs carry the lonely to peaceful sleep, and none can answer.

Darkness falls and brings the rain. A wing tickles my ear, my cheek. A starling flitting by, running from the drizzle. Without thought, I follow. Left and right, over the gutters, 'round and 'round. Finally, it lands upon a shoulder. I see you, a lone eel in the city's pipes, slithering through slick shadowed streets. The percussion of the rain and clouds my steps as I slither after. We cross the borough, to the eastern edge.

I see the burnt chapel, one from long ago, a place we explored once while young. Lines of birds cover the damp bones of the building and shift against the moonlit sky. You enter, moving through charred benches to the half of the building that still stands. You climb the ladder to the attic where the old piano slumbers.

After I ascend, I watch you as you sit. Your gloves and coat come off, then your scarf and stockings.

When you speak, you do not turn to me. *I've missed you.*

Then you light the lamp. No words or songs leave you or me. The wind nuzzles the windows, and the droplets kiss the roof as I discover your new home and new bones. The sort I never hoped to see.

On the tables, goblets hold the dregs of blood. All along the walls, fingers, arms, and wrists, chopped in pieces and arranged like chords. Hazel eyes—yours—on the ground like forgotten crumbs, and bones enough for twenty xylophones. They rest on beds of scarlet corsets and embroidered suits and silk shirts and a very grand wig.

And on you, new lips, neck, eyes, toes, and fingers.

Befuddlement, more than terror, more than grief, hugs my tongue. I ask you where she is, and that is when your tears flow.

At night, we walked the city road, returning here to home,
The clouds above did cry, a thorough shower in the gloam.
Then, far too fast for slick, dark streets: a carriage through the storm.
We could not jump in time before it crushed her like a worm.
And as I held her, screaming, wailing,
The hellish sight my soul impaling,
The carriage door threw wide, a thud,
To scold me for the spray of blood.

Eloquence abandons me, along with my heart. I cannot picture what you say—I don't dare to, lest I fall like snow. Though my tongue is silent, yours is still a whip, ready to crack.

They bade me move. "It is quite vital,
That we attend the Grand Recital."
Others passed, and though I cried,
Not one more carriage pulled aside.
Men I played with, men who paid me,
Not a one would stop to aid me.
To the theater, off they went,
Leaving me in my lament.
They sat there, marveled at the stage,
While with my hands, I dug a grave.
The music swirled around the rich,
As she lay rotting in a ditch.

Your mismatched fingers curl then, turning white, and the most frightening hunger of all burns within you, scorching me. I've seen that hunger in the wolves, in the thieves, in the rippers.

Such souls do not deserve to hear it.
I will not rest until I steal it.
'Til then I'll not know peaceful sleep.
Listen to my tones and weep.

You sit, then, at the piano, and you play, and I shake with the wood under my feet. These new parts of you have brought new skills, years of mastery that are not your own, and they are so beautiful. Too beautiful. Skulls and skeletons chatter on the quaking floor, a thunder of rotted applause. The birds outside swoop down and tap the windows. Throw themselves against the glass.

You sing. It hurts. Pounding piano and warbling birds, tapping feet slamming down, down, down. Demons dance upon these walls, and I fear you. I fear you, and though our faces are one, I do not recognize you.

I fear you, until I see your new eyes, choked by tears. Blue as morning in the new springtime. Blue as the sapphires the high women wear.

Blue as the necklace nestled in the hollow of your throat.

I remember then.

We two, thrown out by the one who built our bones, made to live with birds in the bloody shadows. We two, joining those birds in ripping through the skin of the trees and the earth, and gnashing wriggling grubs for food. We two, curled in cradles of mud, our ribs forming xylophones on our sides. We two, weeping to know the barest kiss of a sunbeam.

Her, your only light.

And I hear it now, your music, ringing.

I understand your cries, your singing.

And why you've turned these men to bones and turned this attic into home.

We toiled, labored without voice, bloody work our only choice.

We watched high houses laugh and scorn and punish us for being born.

And here among these cold, dark streets,

We barely stayed upon our feet.

Is it any wonder, then, who you turned out to be?

What else were you to do, my friend, but copy what we see?

They kill, they crush, they grind to dust, and all of it for greed and lust.

But you have killed for love.

In this, I see that you are right.

They shouldn't get to have that light.

The music fades once again as your fingers leave the keys and your back hunches, spine curling like a fallen leaf. I step over clothes and corpses and hold you against my heart. So many nights were we each other's only warmth, and once again, we intertwine in shivering grief.

You beg me not to leave you, and I promise I will never. I wonder in a whisper why it wasn't enough to rob them of life. I wonder why you've taken these parts for yourself—for what you've stolen, you do not use. No circus stage or parlor, no king's hall or lowly alleyway vibrates with the symphony you've paid this price to pen. And why?

It is still a gift, and it cannot be lost. It is still a gift, and it must be mine, and it must be perfect, you cry, so beautifully. *For the woman who deserved it most. It must be perfect, to cross the realms and bring her spirit home to me.*

I understand. Our mournful tangle lasts until the morning birds tap upon the window. I tell you where my path goes next and wish you love and fond farewell. What coppers I can spare, if any, will be yours. Down the ladder, through the pews, and back upon the muddy streets. Accompanied only by the fading tears of the storm, I cross the river and leave the birds and bones with you.

My existence begins in earnest then. I dance in the clean streets, and the parlors and recital halls. Some nights, I cross back, and we drink and dine. I tell you of my life and loves, and the silly things people care about in Inner Sternham. You tell me of the children you teach, those who now live safely under your wing. I learn letters and share them with you. You find more birds and share them with me.

On tiny slips tied to tiny talons, I write where the music lives, where it will visit.

I confess, I go to listen, for I know they'll never play again after my sparrows reach you. And as I bathe in what will be their final curtain calls, I feel you in the tunnels below the streets, your ravenous reverence tickling my soles. I see you in the bodies you string over streetlamps, warnings to the wealthy.

One by one, month by month, the city birds fall and the city bones break.

Recital halls soon bar their doors and windows,

parlor locks are turned, troupes and circuses take long routes to avoid our city. Your lips change again, your eyes too, and the chords in your fingers are rearranged once, twice, too many times to count. *Better than the last. Yes, almost perfect.*

Before long, the people across the river and in the high houses know silence, their clocks and church bells caked with rust, their hymnals bathed in dust. Tarnished flutes and forsaken pianos are dumped near the Blighted Borough. Beggars' homes become recital halls and unwanted children know music from the time they can toddle. I'm no longer paid to dance—no matter, I've trained the birds, and they fetch me coppers, jewels.

You have done what you wished: brought high houses into silence. They know now that only those within our lowly caste can hum and strum and still know the warm caress of the next sunrise.

One song yet lives near those mansions cold and mute. One loving elegy begins to ring whenever the finely cobbled streets grow dark and someone, a foolish little someone, thinks they're safe to sing.

The xylophone bones go tink, tink, tink.

THE BRIEF UNMOURNED DEATH OF ANTON KAMINSKI

M.E. Wilczek

ANTON'S CHEEK SPLIT against the ladder as he fell, Casey Elligan's hands around his ankles. Bee dropped from the other end of the monkey bars and shoved Casey away from him. "Quit it! Can't you see he's hurt?"

Casey sprawled on the wood chips and snarled, showing her teeth. "He's *dead*, idiot, haven't you ever seen somebody die before?"

Bee hadn't, actually. "Are you sure?" She prodded the body with her foot. She was thinking of it as *the body* and not *Anton,* which was probably a sign that Casey was right.

The thing that had been Anton five minutes ago was flopped against the ladder with its head twisted back and to the left, and she could see blood where his cheek had met the metal rung of the ladder. As she poked, his arm fell limply forward in a position that would have been very uncomfortable, had he still been Anton and not merely a body. She turned on Casey, who was checking her shirt for blood. "You killed him."

Casey waved her hand, dismissing Bee's condemning tone. "It was an accident, obviously. We were playing." She pushed up and jogged toward the fence, to report the death. There were just two monitors assigned to the whole playground, and these two liked to flirt more than they liked looking at the children running feral. They hadn't noticed a thing.

The sun baked Bee's shoulders as she squatted next to the body. She'd always wondered what it would look like. D*eath.* She wondered if this was Anton's first. Without conscious thought, she reached toward the base of Anton's skull, where short curled hairs camouflaged the incision scar from when his save file had been implanted. She hoped it hadn't been damaged by the blow.

A shadow cooled her neck. "You're not supposed to touch that," Casey said.

Bee knew that. Everyone knew that. But of course Casey thought she was so smart. "You could have damaged his file. That was really dumb, Casey."

"Oh no, they'd have to restore him from backups and he'd lose a whole five minutes."

"It was really dumb."

"I've seen a bunch of them. Dies. I saw my brother twice." Casey sat on the hot tarmac and picked at the sand at the edge of an anthill. "I think he's getting nicer every time, actually. I hope he dies again."

"Your brother is not getting nicer. He's the same, that's the whole point."

"I know what I know. He's getting nicer." An ant clambered up and over the rim of the anthill, and Casey mashed it with her thumb. Grinning, she reached over and wiped the ant parts on Bee's shirt.

"Get away!" Bee backed up, but didn't leave. There was no way she was leaving before the extraction team arrived. "I wish *you* would get nicer."

Casey swept the anthill flat, sending the grains skimming across the blacktop and laying out a smooth canvas of sand. Then she lay flat herself and closed her eyes. "Maybe I should die."

The extraction team arrived before recess was even done, pulling up in their black car and their black uniforms.

The minders pointed towards Bee and Casey—or, more likely, towards the thing that used to be Anton—and the extraction team hustled up to the monkey bars.

"Get back, kids," said the tallest one. Casey opened her eyes, sat up, and scooched about four inches farther away from the body, but both girls stayed to watch. There were five extractors on the team, but you couldn't see any of their faces behind their mirrored helmets. The one who was talking wasn't doing much of it—he had no questions for them. Bee wanted Casey to get in trouble for pulling Anton down, but since they didn't ask, she didn't squeal.

The extractors propped the body up against the ladder that had broken Anton's neck and did a perfunctory vitals check. Then Bee saw a glint of metal as the extractor who seemed to be in charge pulled a blade from his belt and pressed it to the seam on Anton's neck. There was no blood.

"Not his first death," Casey said too loudly, proud of knowing everything.

The chief extractor looked at her sharply and snapped. "It *was*, actually. They modified infant surgeries ten years ago, and now even for originals it's an easy extract. Reduces trauma, works great."

Casey went redder than usual, but she kept her smile held tight. "I guess my brother was too old for a clean seam. I've seen him die twice. So far."

The extractor shook his head and turned back to his work. "I'm sorry you had to see that. And this."

"I don't mind. It's interesting."

The extractor pulled a small plastic-looking black square from Anton's neck and tucked it into a pocket on his uniform. Then he stood and signaled his teammates, who pulled the corpse from where it lay and folded it to be carried back to the waiting extractor car.

After the team had gone, Bee stared at the dark red smear that had been left on the ladder. Then Casey was climbing back up the ladder and nearly lost her footing as her sandal skidded through the stain. The terror of a potential second fall startled Bee to attention.

Casey caught Bee thinking too hard. "He'll be back tomorrow, dummy." She reached out her red-stained sandal sole toward Bee and Bee finally walked away.

"All green?" asked one of the bored monitors as Bee passed.

"Grass green," she answered mechanically, "Just have to pee."

When she was alone in the bathroom stall, Bee prodded the back of her neck, and there it was. The short raised scar was puckered together with transparent floss, and if it was cut away they could take out her soul.

***

Bee slipped downstairs after bedtime that night and took a glass of water and a fruit knife from the kitchen. Back in the hallway bathroom, she found a hand mirror in one of the drawers and held her hair away from her neck, twisting as she tried to get a good look. There it was, just like Anton's: two fleshy lips pursed together and bound by clear twine looping across the seam. She went to retrieve the knife and realized she'd need a hair tie. Or a third hand, but she thought that was less likely to helpfully appear in her bathroom.

There was a soft knock on the bathroom door. *Shave-and-a-hair-cut.* Mom.

"Sorry, Mom, I didn't mean to wake you up. Just getting some water."

"In the bathroom?"

"No, I—" She tucked the fruit knife into her waistband and opened the door. Mom was in the hallway wearing a robe, holding it closed with her arms folded across her body, cheeks pink. She didn't look sleepy, but she did look annoyed. The door to her parents' room was ajar. "I couldn't find a hair tie. It's hot."

Mom wordlessly reached into the drawer Bee had just been searching, pulled out a hair tie, and held it up between them. Bee flushed and took it. "Now go back to bed. Sleep is important for a growing girl."

Back in her room, Bee pulled her hair up into a side ponytail and felt along the stitches. *What am I doing?* She couldn't get the image of Anton out of her head. A little black square of plastic. And tomorrow he'd be back, in a brand-new shell.

Carefully, she put the knife to the first stitch. The thread resisted for a moment, then sprang loose. The next one was easier—when she put the knife to it, the thread pulled loose through the tiny holes in her skin. She set the knife on the table and pulled at the string with her fingers. It slid silkily and slightly wet with sweat, reminding Bee of slurping a long noodle.

All at once the stitches were undone, and a three-inch length of floss dangled, tickling Bee's neck. The mouth of her seam gaped open. Bee pushed the lips apart and felt inside, not knowing what to expect, and found a dry fold of skin ending in a hard plastic lump. Bee wondered if she would die were she to remove it. *If I do, I'll have saved them the trouble of retrieving my file.* Bee took a deep breath, pinched at the plastic, and pulled.

She didn't die, at least not immediately. And she was still conscious. She stared at the thing in her hand. It did look just like Anton's. Black, plastic casing, a thin square less than two inches long. She weighed it in her palm. Lighter than a Triscuit. One side of the square, the edge she'd grasped to pull it out, was slightly bulbous. She moved closer to the window to see if the moonlight might offer better illumination. She flipped the device over, and everything looked strange in the gentle glow, but she didn't want to turn her light on and get in trouble with Mom. She thought the underside might be slightly shiny—some kind of contact pad?—but then her own skin looked a little shiny in this light, too: colorless and gray.

The lighting changed, then, to a red pulse that rapidly grew brighter and closer. Out the window, there was a black extractor car creeping up the street without a sound, the throbbing light signaling that an emergency was at hand.

Bee knew that they were coming for her. They must have gotten an alert of some kind when her save file came out, but still she begged the universe to let them drive past her house and go somewhere else.

But they didn't.

***

Two uniformed extractors exited the car. The one who'd been driving said something to his partner, who nodded and pulled a walkie talkie from their belt, and Bee heard a burst of static.

The two extractors walked up to Bee's front door and the driver reached for the bell. The other agent angled their head up, scanning the windows, and Bee pulled back into her room. *Ding-dong.*

Bee rushed back to her bed and hid the knife under her mattress before pulling the covers up and fumbling at the back of her neck. She tried to

jam the save file back into its cavity. Was it right side up? She could hear her parents bumbling in their room, and her dad thumping down the stairs. He opened the door to the extractors and Bee could hear words floating up: "lost contact" and "wellness check" and "sorry."

Then there were footsteps coming and Bee knew she had to pretend to be asleep. She tried again to push her file back home into the port in her neck but a springy resistance kept pushing it back into her fingers, and suddenly Mom was at the door.

Shave-and-a-hair-cut.

Bee pulled her hand away from her neck and closed her eyes tight. She was sleeping! She had been sleeping the whole time. She heard the door creak open.

She heard another shrill burst of static and she screwed her eyes shut. If she was asleep, she couldn't have done anything that would get her in trouble. Another burst of static startled her eyes open and she dimly saw the figures of the grownups in her room. There were the two extractors—one quite close and looming over her—their uniforms covering every inch of their bodies. There was her mother, shrugging her pink robe around her hunched shoulders. The moonlight illuminated where her face should be and it shone gray and smooth and featureless, reflecting the still-pulsing red light from the extractors' car. One of the extractors stepped up to Bee, then, and as a scratchy canvas glove tipped her head to expose the back of her neck, she knew he was looking at the save file half-flopping out of her.

"Someone's cut her seam, see? It must have popped out when she rolled over in her sleep."

A burst of static.

"You'd be surprised. Kids can be awful. There was an incident at her school today, a boy got pulled off the monkey bars and had to be regenned. She didn't say anything about it?"

A series of staccato static bursts. Bee's face was pressed into her pillow, held there by the officer, and she couldn't see the mannequin huddled in her mother's robe.

"We might be looking at a bullying problem. We'll check into it, ma'am." He pushed at Bee's neck with expert fingers. "For tonight, we'll re-insert this. Tell her to stay away from the bullies at school. I think the girl's name was . . . what was it, Kelsey?"

A burst of static came from a different part of the room.

"Right, *Casey*," he said. Bee felt her file catch, and stay in place. Her nose was still pressed against the pillow. Every breath was hot and close and drew the cotton against her nostrils.

"We don't have to reset her, do we?" Bee's mother asked. Now Bee let her eyes snap open and stay wide. There Mom was, standing at the window, robe wrapped around her, shoulders still hunched, only now she had a nose right where it should be, and frown lines by her mouth, and that weird hair on her chin. Her eyes flicked from the officer to Bee and she smiled—wide. "Bee! Are you all right, my love?"

***

The following day, Bee pocketed safety scissors during her second period art class and found a quiet corner of the playground at recess. Stay away from bullies, the extractor had said. Especially that Casey, said "Mom."

The extractors had looped new thread through her seam before they left last night. She knew that what she'd seen *had* to be wrong. The images seemed murky. Very different from the clarity of memory. She could recall Anton's fall in perfect vivid detail—Casey's laughter, his yelp, the crunch of impact. But when she thought about her mother in the moonlight, it was just a flash. When she tried to zoom in on the details—which hand was on top as she clasped her robe? was she barefoot?—she couldn't pan and zoom, like in a real memory. It had to be a dream.

Bee saw the school nurse walking Anton out onto the playground. Bee scowled at herself for doubting if that was really the boy she knew. It *was* Anton. That was Anton. She could see it was Anton. He even had the same dumb uneven bangs from where his mom cut his hair. The regen was perfect. He saw Bee looking at him and started walking over.

Suddenly Bee's head was jerked sideways, and Bee looked up to see Casey smiling as she let go of her handful of Bee's hair. "See? He's back and green as grass. Told you." Bee shoved Casey without a word, got up, and started heading back toward the school building.

Bee couldn't avoid walking past Anton, but she could avoid speaking to him, and she did. She pretended for the monitors that she needed the bathroom.

In the privacy of the stall, she found her seam again, the one the extractors had looped with new thread before leaving last night. She couldn't wait until she got home. She pulled out her scissors.

Snip. Snip. Snip. It was easier this time, now that she knew what she was doing. She prodded at the edge of the file. It had alerted the extractors last night when she took it out. If she removed it again, she wondered how long she would have before they came storming into the school.

She pocketed the scissors and returned outside. Casey found her immediately, throwing her weight on Bee's shoulders in a hug that wasn't friendly.

"Your *boyfriend's* back," she said, "aren't you going to go kiss him?"

"I saw." Bee needed to find a quiet spot to pop out her file without anyone noticing, and of all the people she didn't want to see, Casey was number one. She tried to shake her off, but she was hanging off Bee's shoulders like a monkey baby clinging to mama.

"Are you ready to admit that he's fine yet?"

"Yes."

"So you can't be mad at me anymore," Casey insisted.

"I can do what I want."

Casey scowled at that, and let go of Bee. Then, looking her right in the eyes, she grabbed a handful of Bee's long hair and pulled as hard as she could. Bee's head was yanked down so hard her knee buckled and she almost fell to the ground.

"Hey!"

"You're mean."

Bee protested. "*You* just pulled *my* hair. How am *I* mean?"

"You have to make up. We had a fight, but everything is okay, and you have to forgive me."

"You didn't even say you were sorry!"

"Well, I'm not sorry. It was an accident. Anton is fine. What's there to be sorry for?"

"You killed him!" Bee pushed Casey away. "Leave me alone. Mom said I'm not even supposed to talk to you."

Casey sneered. "Oh, is that how it is? Your *mom* said? Have to listen to your *mom*, don't you, you baby?"

I'm not a baby. And my mom might not be my mom. "Leave me alone." If Bee repeated herself, maybe Casey would get bored and leave. Bee turned her back on the other girl and tried to walk toward the big maple tree at the edge of the playground. She could sit against its trunk and hide the back of her neck for a few minutes.

But Casey had Bee's hair in her fist again and she was pulling, a few strands being torn from their roots. "Baby! Don't run away, baby, you might get a boo-boo."

Bee twisted back toward Casey, but Casey still had Bee's hair, and the torque of her pulling shifted the position of Bee's unsecured seam. She could feel the two planes of skin moving against each other inside her neck in a way that felt wrong. "Let go!" She grabbed at Casey's shoulder, at her shirt and hair, clawing at her earlobe with her fingernail, and the girls fell squalling to the ground.

Casey had Bee pinned in the patchy, pebbly dirt. With one hand she pulled at Bee's hair again, thumping the back of her head against the dusty ground, and with the other hand she scrabbled for a fistful of soil, which she then ground against Bee's cheek and tried to force into her mouth. "Stop fighting! Fighting isn't nice!" Casey teased, pressing sandy loam against Bee's lips and up into Bee's nose. She let up with her other hand then just enough to slam Bee's head back down onto the dirt, jostling the open cavity at Bee's nape.

Bee howled and let go of Casey's hair, grasping wildly at her attacker, trying to find a strong enough hold so she could get the upper hand and pull free. *She's going to kill me.* Bee saw Casey's smile, the bright red scratch across her face, the glob of snot streaked across her cheek that Casey didn't even seem to know was there. Casey pounded Bee's head against the dirt again and again, and Bee felt her file shift and squish against her moving flesh. And then she felt it come free.

A new thought, much scarier than death: *She's going to damage my file.*

Bee screamed and clawed at Casey and finally she had hold of her shoulder and yanked, catching her off guard and throwing her off balance, but she still had hold of Bee's hair. Casey looked wild and spit-flecked and relentless, but besides Casey, besides the fight, something was terribly wrong.

Bee's own hands were too pale.

Bee scanned wildly for the playground monitors—hadn't they noticed there was a fight?—and saw two gray, faceless mannequins leaning in toward each other where Miss Garber and Miss Pill should be. Bee screamed for help, but she couldn't hear her own voice. Everything sounded like static.

Over on the playground, a dummy wearing Anton's clothes looked over, angling the smooth planes where its face should be first to the girls in the dirt, and then to the fence where the monitors stood. He slid down the slide and walked toward them, in no particular hurry. Around him, children and dummies played indiscriminately, some laughing and talking, some chittering in staccato static screams.

Casey bashed Bee's head against the ground again and cackled as she regained the upper hand, and a drop of blood fell on Bee's face. Did Bee have a face? Bee swiped cold plastic fingers against a featureless smooth plane and knew she was among the dead.

She wouldn't be free until Casey no longer had a grip on her hair. Bee stopped clawing at the animal that was Casey and scrabbled for the scissors in her pocket, desperately snapping them at her hair in an attempt to cut herself free.

"Ow!" Bee had caught a finger in the blades. Casey let go, and Bee was free. She stood over Casey, a horrible and bloody child scowling and clutching at wounded fingers, howling out curses she shouldn't have known. Bee tried to curse back—*balls! piss!*—but her own voice was static and the blood on Casey's fingers was not revenge enough.

Bee grabbed at Casey's head and pushed her face in the dirt, shoving her pink fleshy nose up against an anthill where marching soldiers trod in and out bringing food to their queen, and Casey's dripping string of snot drooled across their sandy fortress. Casey was flat on her stomach, and Bee had her knee firmly on her back holding her down. Bee could hear the children on the playground yelling at her to stop, and the approaching converging static of the mannequins who thought they were real. Casey grappled wildly at Bee, trying to pull her off, but Bee was chopping at her hair, and at the thread on her seam. She slid her lifeless fingers into the nape of Casey's neck and then she held Casey in her hands: a black square of plastic,

which she threw into the woods as hard as she could. Casey was squalling and cursing, squealing for a monitor, and when Bee let up on the pressure in her knee, Casey rolled over and saw Bee's smooth gray face and the mannequin monitors approaching, and that's when she lost her words and really started to scream.

AN EXCERPT FROM A FEAST OF PUTRID DELIGHTS

Valentina Rojas

WHEN YOU THINK about it, delusion is the first thing diagnosed at the doctor's office. *Everything's fine! There's nothing to worry about. Everyone experiences sleepless years like this.*

It's no use.

I've rehearsed my own story—the story that everything is alright—and am trying to explain this to the doctor when he stops me mid-sentence.

"How long have you gone without sleeping?"

"Let's see. Last full night of sleep was two days ago. But it isn't—"

He cuts me off again.

"When did this start?"

I blink.

Blue and red lights. A ringing in my ears. Bodies shuddering to the ground.

"Six years ago, I think."

"Right."

"On and off," I add, to lessen the severity.

"Hmm, I see. Well, I'm going to prescribe you some Ambien. Take one tonight and catch up on sleep. I'll recommend you to a sleep physician if it doesn't help, but let's give the old college try first. Okay?"

His question doesn't warrant an answer.

Before I know it, I'm scooted out of the room by the doctor's invisible hands to the receptionist's corner, to wait and pay the copay fee, then back into my hot-junk of a car.

No time to admit to the good doctor that this sleeplessness has been going on for years and that sometimes weeks go by without a wink of sleep. No time to tell him I'm *unnaturally* unwell. And, no time to protect myself against the consequences if he *does* end up believing me.

I crinkle the prescription into the glove compartment, where it joins a lifetime of wadded-up, unused scripts. Could make a good side buck selling these. I look in the rearview mirror and shake my head. I promised not to do that anymore.

Another dead end.

I jam the key into the ignition and tear off into the serpentine highway.

The last good sleep I had was almost the death of me.

I was working at a little joint called Comma. Your typical, new-age chef nightmare. A historic creaky house-turned brunch spot, at the corner of Ellum and some new block of gentrified apartments overlooking a dirty dog park.

I'd start weekend mornings at 4 am, prepping containers of cyst-colored hollandaise sauce until I could smell it sweating out of my pores, and chopping fine potatoes (they had to be "fine" to validate the elevated dining prices) until Binder, a gruff New Jersey implant, appeared, breathing the odd critique down my neck.

Yuppies and college kids gathered at the door in large, fleshy bulges, waiting for a seat on our cramped patio. Plate after plate of glacial eggs, sausage links, and that damn hollandaise sauce zooming by us. We all turned a sick shade of puce by noon.

When our shifts ended, whoever wasn't on clean-up duty went looking for distractions for whoever wanted to pass the evening away. And naturally, I'd tag along—bored, expendable, the restless venom of youth pumping through my veins.

This evening in particular, I had no other place to go. Mika and I weren't speaking at the time. My aunt Jo was in Florida getting some experimental cancer treatment. So when Rody and Binder asked me to join them at their loft, I was game.

Binder's loft was a bright-white room on the second floor of a hipster development, sandwiched between a tattoo parlor and a noisy bar. Pretty generic all in all. Inside the elevator, a fresh paint smell lingered and I felt us all sharing a pre-high on our way up.

The narrow hallway of Binder's loft gave way to a messy bachelor pad. Mismatched IKEA furniture, a bulky record player, a collection of vintage framed t-shirts framed the unmounted television. The glass coffee table, with its marbled green base and spotless surface, was anachronistic, which spoke to an intentionality not apparent elsewhere in the room.

Rody swept his dark hair into a ponytail and knelt onto the faded rug. While we settled in, Binder went off and I heard the static hum of a television somewhere in the kitchen. Binder's hacks echoed against the industrial walls until he reappeared, his lumpy figure wobbling over to us with a plastic baggie tucked between two sausage fingers.

"Ladies first."

I didn't want to be a coward, so I pushed the apprehension out of my mind and snatched the baggie. There was a performative aspect to this ritual I enjoyed more than the drug itself. The placing, the camaraderie, and the instant moans of otherworldly escape shared among the participants. That and boredom, like I said—craving something to make the hours go by quickly.

I shook out two lines for each of us, which elicited a nod of approval from Rody, and a clap from Binder, who kept insisting this was proof he wasn't a "cheapo". Perched over the heavy glass, I snorted, instantly erasing the world around me. The capillaries on my cheeks felt flushed with new blood. Binder's laugh echoed around us. They both hit the lines in unison, letting out a gasp I knew only a few had heard before. Then my nose tickled

something awful. Like an allergy attack gone mad.

The last thing I heard before blacking out was Binder whispering, *"fuck,"* as his large torso thudded to the ground.

I woke up days later to the sound of Mika's voice on the tail end of a phone call.

"Binder's fine. He's getting his stomach pumped but he'll live. Rodrigo too. The idiots."

"Good," I whispered hoarsely.

He turned to me, mouth gaped open like a fish. "I got to go, honey."

In spite of my grin, everything hurt.

I could feel his lips on the hummingbird flutter of my eyelids as he leaned in. A kiss on each eye. My body went rigid.

He told me the gist of it while we adjusted my bed: the cocaine was laced with a new street drug. Something the kids called *Cloud*—a sedative some yuppie drop-outs had unleashed onto the market. On its own, it wasn't deadly, but in combination, weird shit happened.

A nurse swung by with a plate of goopy-looking food, admonishing me in an old southern tone about how I was lucky to be alive. I didn't want a lecture, so I just nodded along.

At the sight of the food, my stomach growled. I unsheathed a plastic spoon while Mika went on.

The drug part didn't interest me back then. At least, not in the way he assumed.

"Wait—you're saying I *slept*?"

"Yes, for two days."

I dove into the pudding cup.

"Mika! This is . . . "

My eyes burned from crying.

"I thought that whole thing was under control."

"If you think sleeping a full night every few weeks is under control, then sure."

"And the doctors? I mean, have you ever been to a specialist?"

"This is why I didn't tell you. Doctors aren't wizards, you know. Plus, they'll just think I'm a freak. Get all lab rat on me."

"So you have been . . . ?"

I rolled my eyes at him and scooped another mouthful of pudding into my mouth. The light cocoa flavor was replaced with a thick, congealed sludge. A combination of lard and that pink paste you get at the dentist's office. I couldn't swallow it, not after that smell; sewage cake and old menstrual blood. I spit it out on the plate and pushed the tray away.

"This shit is *rotten*."

Mika smirked.

"What did you expect? It's hospital food, *Chef*."

Except I wasn't *Chef* back then, and Mika liked to tease. It was something we daydreamed about. Well, Mika did, anyway. I hitched my dream alongside his, because it made sense. Because I was desperately trying to find an obsession we could share.

He handed me the juice box, which didn't quite taste like apple, and did little to rid my tongue of the unpleasant residue.

For a moment, expired food aside, it felt like the old days. The days before culinary school and the adventures of Mika and his shiny new fiancé. A little too much like the old days. I watched Mika's gentleness grow smaller in his eyes when his phone pinged, a message from his fiancé surely. Might as well change the subject.

"Do you know where I could get some of that Cloud stuff?"

"You gotta be fucking kidding me."

"To sleep! Sleep!"

Mika went on a tirade about having had to convince the nurses I was clean as a baby and would never have done that unless I was influenced, which I was prone to, and that rehab was not necessary. They couldn't force me,

anyway, so they laid off after his explanation of my weak and gullible character.

"Don't do this to me again."

"No promises. The food here is pretty great." That was a couple of months before Aunt Jo would pass, before I would quit Comma and leave bad habits behind, before Mika and I would open Iris together, and three years to the day after Pixel happened.

I thought about Cloud for a bit, I'll admit. But whatever had started in California died there, and after a series of crackdowns, Cloud was another fantastical magic dream needing to remain in the past.

Plus, I swore to myself I'd ditch the substances on my nighttime escapades, not on account of any moral reasoning, really. The thing about them was they made the lies hard to control, harder to recall, and I couldn't risk that. I was lucky enough that my first hospitalization happened with Binder and Rody, who had as much to lose as I did. So *Comma* became the end to a chapter, a scapegoat for a problem no one knew of. No harm, no foul. The same couldn't be said of Mika, being my closest friend, but at least I could keep a lid on how bad it really was.

DO YOU BELIEVE IN MISTER BONES?

BELIEVE IN MISTER BONES

a novel by

Max Booth III

DO YOU BELIEVE IN MISTER BONES?

AN UNKNOWN COMPELLING FORCE

Melissa Nowark

IT'S EASY TO see why the area we currently tread upon is called Dead Mountain. The local Mansi people call it *Kholat Syakhl*, which can be translated directly to *silent mountain*, or *dead peak*. The land is truly dead. There are no trees, the land is barren, and I haven't seen an animal for miles. As we set up our campsite, it's eerie how quiet it is. The whooshing of my blood as it soars past my eardrums sounds like a passing train as we finish mounting the tent.

What's not easy to see, however, is how nine experienced hikers met such grisly ends. Many theories exist surrounding Dyatlov Pass, ranging from an avalanche to aliens, but no single theory can explain all of their brutal injuries. Justine and I disagree on how they may have ultimately met their end, but we agree on one thing: it took them by surprise. The oven was set up, some weren't even wearing shoes, and there was a gash in the tent, which later on was discovered to have originated from the inside. They weren't ready for whatever drove them to their deaths.

As much as we wanted to experience the full Dyatlov experience, being from the Southern United States, we decided to visit during the spring, after the thaw. Regardless of the weather, after having studied this place for years, being here is surreal.

Tent set up, I start taking photos of the desolate landscape while Justine counts provisions. "Babe, we're okay," I reassure her. She's already inventoried twice since we've arrived. I understand her anxiety; we're here alone, farther out than we've ever been. I'm nervous too, but with more of a giddy excitement that I can't contain. I've been looking forward to this for so long.

She looks at me and smiles, a dimple forming on her left cheek. "I know, Edie, it's not going to disappear if I turn around," she says, though she still takes one last look at the bottled water, which makes me laugh. "Come on, enough seriousness; let's explore."

The sun is bright overhead as we slowly examine the perimeter of our campsite. Even though it's officially spring here, there's still a slight chill in the air, but the sun warms my face. There's a slight breeze that cools me off whenever I get too warm, the weather regulating me to the perfect temperature. The perfect sun. The perfect breeze. Why is everything so dead?

"Keep track of the direction we're going in, so it's an easy walk home," Justine says, as I snap photo after photo of the dismal landscape. "It's not a secret how they got so lost from their campsites. With zero visibility, I'm not sure I could find my own toes."

Justine grabs the camera and gets a closeup of me covering my eyes from the sun, which is directly over my head now. My cheeks are slightly reddened from the blazing rays. "All of your photos were going to be the same; now there's something beautiful in the mix.

***

We met in the classic, old-fashioned way—in a college bar. We majored in dramatically different subjects, but we were both interested in the weird, the unusual. I was a history major, combing through books to find the strange, while Justine was a biology major, the human body her bizarre interest. I was shocked to hear that she had not only heard of Dyatlov Pass, but had read about it at length. We were those queers in the corner of the bar, cheeks blushed from alcohol, arguing over the gruesome fates of nine Russian hikers from sixty-five years prior.

I don't believe in love at first sight, but it didn't take long before we were nose to nose in bed, listening to Tegan and Sara while we simultaneously caressed each other's faces.

***

As it gets darker, the wind picks up, and we quickly make our way back to the campsite. We chose a spot close to the water, the only real landmark in this area. I try not to remember that a body was pulled out of this water. A body missing a tongue.

Despite the pleasant afternoon breeze, the cold at night is brutal. We brought plenty of blankets, but we scoot closer together. Besides the warmth radiating off of Justine, there's a glow to her face that makes me fall in love with her all over again.

"What are you smiling about, solnishko?" she asks as she pulls my hair out from the back of my jacket. Little sun. Her touch is soft and warm; familiar.

"You," I reply. I hold the back of her neck and bring her in for a slow, loving kiss. She tastes of mint and chamomile tea. She tastes like home. She unzips my sleeping bag and cuddles in next to me. We're so tangled together, it's hard to tell where I end and Justine begins. I shiver in anticipation as she runs her fingers along my neck, my collarbone. There's soft light from the moon overhead shining through the mesh in the tent. It makes her skin look ethereal, her brown eyes like swirls of cream in coffee. Her cold hands start pulling through the layers of clothing I've piled on. It's freezing outside, yet my face is hot. Every time she touches the dimples of my back, I forget we're in a dead, cold landscape in the mountains of Russia.

***

I am unaware that I've fallen asleep. My eyes open to the most wondrous colors I've ever seen. Pink, purple, green. I shake my head, trying to place where I am. The colors disappear and I'm once again shrouded in darkness. It's pitch black; even though I know the moon is still hanging overhead, it's almost as if something has hidden it.

I turn, shivering, and realize my sleeping bag is still unzipped. Although I can't see an inch in front of me, I know Justine is dead asleep. Her little snores and snuffles fill the void inside the tent. I hear a voice; it's unfamiliar and speaking clear English, without any hint of an accent.

I turn my head back and forth to pinpoint the location of the sound. It's coming from everywhere and nowhere all at once. It's inside my head, yet outside of time and space itself. It's almost as if God themself is acknowledging my presence. I rub my eyes, trying to blink away the darkness. When I open them again, I'm dazzled by the brightness in the tent. It's not morning—this light is not daylight. This light is unnatural, uncomfortable, like being in a supermarket on a stormy day. A flash strikes my vision, and I turn around to see Justine, a knife held high above her head and a sick smile crawling across her face; her once chocolate eyes now black as coal . . .

I wake up in a cold sweat, a scream threatening to escape my throat. I thrash violently, waiting for the knife to come down on my face, and I see that Justine is sleeping soundly. When my vision clears, I notice everything in the tent is tinted a purplish hue, matching the fairy lights in our library at home. I peer glance out of the mesh on the side of the tent.

Purple. In a landscape of nothing but dusky brown and dying green, I see vibrant purple. I've never seen the aurora borealis before, but there's no possible way that's what this is. This isn't artificial light, this isn't a reflection, and this isn't a quirk of the rising sun. Am I awake? Am I still dreaming?

I quietly make my way to the door of the tent, terrified yet curious all the same. Every scrape of the zipper's teeth through the slider sends a jolt up my spine. I poke my head out see something incomprehensible. The purple I'm seeing isn't coming from the sky, but from a solid mass of . . . something, slithering through the river behind our tent. It has a preternatural glow to it that makes me think of radiation, of the grainy footage that came out of Chernobyl. I can't look straight at it. My corneas burn as I try to establish how this mass came to be. It seems to take over the entire landscape.

It stops slithering, detecting my presence. I

hold my breath, waiting to wake up. I have to wake up.

It turns towards me so quickly, I let out a blood curdling scream, my throat feeling like it's cracked open, startling Justine awake. She pulls me into the tent and I land hard on the ground. She grabs her boots and her flashlight as I scream "Don't go, don't go!" She holds me aside as she looks out of the small hole I've left in the tent door.

She's captivated for what feels like hours, but couldn't have been more than a few minutes. When she turns back to me, her face is scrunched up in confusion. "Did you have a bad dream, solnishko?"

I'm still shaking wildly as I grip her hands. "You . . . you didn't see?"

She sighs and any fear she had is replaced by a comforting presence as she scoops my face in her hands. "Lamb, you've just had a bad dream. Go back to sleep."

There's no way I'm going back to sleep. It's not long until the sun rises fully, anyway. I huddle up in the corner of the tent, eyes wide, searching for motion in the dark. I nod off, the adrenaline fizzling out of my bloodstream.

I jolt awake, once again wondering where I am. Justine isn't in the tent, and her sleeping bag isn't warm. She must have gotten up a while ago. I slowly pull open the flap of the tent and begin to shake when I notice Justine is holding a large knife. She looks at me carefully, then laughs when she notices the knife in her hand. "I'm just making breakfast, my sun. I'm sorry you had a bad night. Come and eat."

The fear and anxiety dissolve slowly as I eat breakfast. Justine lovingly jokes about my nightmares; I've always been prone to them, especially in unfamiliar places. As excited as I am to continue studying Dyatlov Pass, the haunting landscape seems to have brought back the night terrors I had as a child. I wonder if the doomed hikers experienced nightmares as well.

I'm enjoying the breakfast stir fry Justine made, but I can't help but notice that there seems to be something off about her. It may just be the sun, but she has a strange aura surrounding her. She looks to be standing in shadow, no matter the sun's position. When I look for the bright glint in her once-beautiful eyes, I see nothing but darkness and dread. Everything goes back to normal so

quickly, I almost believe I've imagined it. Justine's eyes are now full of concern.

"I think I'm going to take a nap," I say to Justine, as I finish washing up after breakfast. "I'm so sleep deprived I'm starting to see things." She follows me into the tent and wraps me up in our blankets, like she would a sick child. "Sleep well, solnishko. I'll be just outside if you need anything."

When I wake up, it's still light outside, but the sun has shifted to the other side of the sky. I've slept longer than I intended. I open the tent flap and begin to call for Justine, but fall silent when I see there's nobody outside. The fire from this morning has fizzled out, smoke drifting towards the river. The wind has picked up once more, and I hear voices under the breeze, chanting. I follow the wind, pulled by a curiosity so strong it has overpowered the fear deep inside my gut. When I reach the river, the voices stop. There's no sign of Justine, but when I look into the rushing water, I notice tiny blue lights floating along the surface. I try to take photos of them, but they come out blurry and grainy, and I'm again reminded of the Chernobyl disaster.

Blood. The word comes so softly I can't be sure where it originated from, but as I look back into the water, the bioluminescent creatures have stalled. The water continues to rush with the wind, but the lights have pooled towards the center of the river, completely still. *Blood.* Something shifts inside me, and suddenly all I want is to give these creatures everything and anything they ask for. My mind feels warped, my own thoughts lost deep inside, fragmenting as they try to make their way to the surface.

I pull the small pen knife out of my pocket and raise it toward my arm when the wind abruptly stops, giving me vertigo. *No.* As I stumble forward, the pen knife falls into the water, but instead of letting it sink to the bottom, the creatures start pushing and pulling until they create an assembly line, sending the knife upriver against the current. I can't believe what I'm seeing—the blue lights are clustered around a angular, but meaty appendage. My eyes refuse to focus and a film begins to cover them, making everything blurry.

Bigger. I look away from the appendage, from the lights, and turn toward our campsite. It's glowing, an unnatural green coming from inside the tent like a beacon. My legs move without being prompted, until I'm pulling up the tent flap. Justine sits inside, tidying up the blankets I threw about during my night terrors. "There you are. I was about to go searching for you, Edie. You can't do that to me," she says, eyes full of love and concern. *Her*.

I sit down in front of Justine, the large kitchen knife I don't remember grabbing glinting under my sleeve. She doesn't flee, she doesn't scream; she's locked in place. Of course my blood won't be enough. I have to sacrifice the person most important to me. It's the only way.

Justine's pupils dilate while I bring the knife back and forth over my fingers, testing its sharpness. Her body remains calm, however, subdued by a supernatural presence. The tip of the knife grazes her lips, and I press one last kiss to the tip of her nose. "You're everything to me," I say, as I use the knife to spread her lips apart, to open her jaw.

The blade comes down on her tongue at an angle, slicing through her taste buds slowly. The blood stains her shirt, her jeans, the blankets we brought from our apartment. The moon has risen, and her blood shines in the light. It gushes through my fingers, sticky. I use my tongue to clean my palm and the handle of the knife. I don't want any of her precious life-blood to go to waste. The metallic taste settles something inside of me—

something yearning, something ancient—but it is not yet satiated.

I inch the blade into Justine's face, just under the dimple I love so much. I pull it towards her neck and sever the carotid artery, blood spraying in all directions. Her blood blotches my skin, my hair, my clothes. I can see in her eyes that she's accepted her fate.

I exit the tent, drenched in the blood of my soulmate. The ultimate sacrifice. I rush towards the river and kneel at the bank, blood still streaming off of me. The instant a droplet hits the rushing water, I come back to myself. Through blood staining my vision, I see a massive, indescribable creature running at me full speed. I feel it slam into my chest and crack the ribs directly surrounding my heart. I close my eyes, knowing there's no surviving this, knowing I sacrificed the only person I loved to the bowels of the earth. The last thing I see before the world goes black is my still beating heart skewered by the  tip of one of the numerous tentacles attached to a being more ancient than the universe itself.

There's something about the river house that calls to Trevor Davis. Moving here will restore him, will fill the hole he can't fill with beer, work, children. But what he gives the land, it takes, and when he discovers a seemingly bottomless sand pit in the yard, his obsession grows to grisly proportions. Part possession story, part body horror, GIVE UNTO US addresses the hole growing deep within us all.

AVAILABLE NOW!

www.Ghoulish.rip

R/FELTGOODCOMINGOUT

Madelyn Lunnen

Popping a 20 yr old blackhead!

Satisfying ear wax removal

You won't believe how long this ingrown hair is!

Sunburn skin peel—super gnarly

I WATCH EACH one of these videos. They're essentially the same thing each time: a part of something being wrenched from its source. Often brutally. I stare transfixed as people snip, tug, and excavate parts of themselves for my entertainment. When I watch these clips, I feel intoxicated. Some people need drugs, alcohol, or God to live. I need these videos. It's like everything is dulled until the moment I start watching someone mutilate their body for me. And then everything comes alive in a heady rush.

I absently pick at a sore on my arm, eyes glued to the screen for the rest of the night.

***

The lunch date was only supposed to be an hour long, but my sister likes to talk, especially when it's about herself. "And I'm thinking that we should do lilacs with ferns for the centerpieces. They just evoke a feeling of love and quiet luxury, you know?" The others nod earnestly. "That's really what I want for this wedding: for people to feel immersed in my and Brody's love, but in a

luxurious way." She says this as if she's Jesus Christ herself, preaching to the starving masses.

I snort and everyone turns to me.

"What is so funny, Delia?" Jess asks, pointedly.

"Well, it's just that your wedding is in October and lilacs won't be in bloom then."

Silence.

And then, the maid of honor desperately blurts out, "I'm sure someone will have them somewhere! It can't be that hard to get lilacs, right?"

I shrug. "I'm sure you're right." After another moment of silence, everyone goes back to discussing the centerpieces and whether or not Jess should fire the bridesmaid who couldn't make it to lunch. Thankfully, I'm saved by a buzzing from my phone. SkinKing posted a new video. The description makes me salivate: *Amy has a pore that she says has been clogged for over ten years!* 🍪 *Numerous doctors have tried and failed to clear it out! Am I up to the task??? Watch as I tackle my trickiest pop yet!!* My skin flushes at the thumbnail: the stretched out, cakey pore on the back of her neck; the surface, gray and cracked. I wonder if it feels as rough as it looks, if it would chafe against my fingertips. How it would feel against my lips. What it would taste like.

I need to watch this video right now.

I jolt up, my chair screeching back, all eyes on me. "I . . . uh . . . have to go to the bathroom." I rush through the restaurant into the restroom. Mercifully, it's empty. I choose the middle stall. I push my earbuds in with one trembling hand as I pull down my pants and underwear with the other. I'm already wet.

But before I can hit play, the door swings open. "Delia?" It's the maid of honor. Courtney, I think?

"Uh, yeah, I'm here."

"Okay, cool, I just need to talk to you when you're done."

I groan. Fuck. I think about what would happen if I turned off my earbuds, hit play with the volume up loud, and picked at my scabs while touching myself. Moving from one sore to another until it was impossible to tell if my fingers were sticky with pus or vaginal fluid. Fuck fuck *fuck*. I can barely control myself. Somehow I resist. I pull my pants up, put my earbuds away, and flush the toilet.

When I come out, she flushes red and squeaks out. "Hey!" She attempts a wave. "I know we haven't met before, but my name is Celia and I'm so excited to be a part of your sister's big day!"

I think she expects me to say something. I remain quiet.

"Anyway, um, this is kind of awkward, but Jess has some concerns? Ummm . . . how do I put this?" She glances at my arms and I know. She's talking about my scabs. The ones I can't stop picking at. At least she can't see what's under my clothes. "It's just that weddings are a big deal and it's important that we all present a gorgeous, unified image. I mean, Margo's even dying her red hair brown!"

"What does that have to do with anything?"

Celia cocks her head, shocked that I don't understand. "So that she doesn't take attention off of Jess, obviously!" She chuckles and reaches into her purse, pulling out several small bottles and a piece of paper. She presses them into my hands, being careful not to touch me. "So listen, I know that skin care can be intimidating! But I've gotten you some samples from the store and I've made a detailed regimen to help you get that bridesmaid glow! Just make sure to apply everything twice a day and call me with any questions! My number is in the Bride Tribe Group Chat!" And then she's out the door.

The meeting drags on for another half hour before Jess dismisses us. When I get home, I watch the video four times in a row. I fall asleep covered in a beautiful mixture of pus, blood, and discharge.

***

He's staring at me from across the bar. I stare back, daring him to approach me. As he nears, I notice that his skin is pockmarked. Three juicy zits sit on his face, like they're waiting for me. I want to squeeze them and lick what dribbles out.

"Hi, my name's Matt. I'm digging your vibe." I've heard variations of this line numerous times. Like always, I pretend to be charmed. "Thanks! My name is D. You're not too bad yourself!"

He laughs. "And how's your night going?"

"It's going okay. Just trying to get laid."

He chokes on his drink. Men aren't used to women being upfront about their sexual needs. In my experience, it's easier this way. I don't want them to think I'm after more than what their body can give me.

"Are you serious?"

"Yes, are you down?"

Matt looks shocked. "I mean, yeah! That's great! Where should we—"

"I rent a room upstairs." I point towards the staircase at the back of the bar. "I'm the second door on the left at the top of the stairs. It's unlocked." Gesturing at the bar, I add, "I'll get us some more drinks and meet you up there in a sec." Matt nods enthusiastically and jogs towards the staircase. He's too horny to consider how sketchy this all feels. With women, I have to work a lot harder to convince them. I go to the bar and order two drinks, dissolving a pill into one of them as I walk upstairs.

Once Matt starts drinking, it only takes a few minutes before he passes out. I'm quivering with excitement as I lean over his face. What will he taste like? He smells earthy, so I imagine his pus will taste similar. I caress his face while I grind against his body. Trailing my tongue around his zits, I wait until I feel like I'm about to explode with want. And then I choose one and bite down, squeezing my teeth around the edges. I feel it burst in my mouth, salty and sublime. I dig my tongue into the hole, lapping up any remnants. Emptying my own sores is incredible, but doing it to somebody else? It's rapturous.

After it's over and I'm satisfied, I lay next to Matt, lost in the afterglow. I scroll Reddit and watch popping videos. But after what I just tasted? They don't feel like enough. So I search out SkinKing's channel and rewatch Amy and her mouth-watering pore. I'd give *anything* to taste it.

When Matt eventually wakes up, I tell him that we had great sex, the best I've had in months. Although he has no memory of what happened, it's clear he wants to believe me. He leaves, and I promise to call him, just as I promise every person brought here. I never call.

***

A few weeks later, we're at an upscale salon browsing bridesmaid dresses. Jess is trying to decide between a purple dress the color of a bruise and a greenish yellowy one reminiscent of pus. The sight of it reminds me of the salty taste of my last cyst. I must've been staring because my sister glares at me, pissed. "What now?"

"Nothing, I just like the green one. It, uh, would be a daring color for a fall wedding . . . and showcase your bold aesthetic?" I'm just cobbling together words I've heard others throw around, but it seems to work.

"You're right, I *do* have a bold aesthetic, and this color would look great against everyone's skin tones," she says. I seriously doubt that, but I do like how the dress makes me feel. When I pinch the fabric, I pretend it's my skin between my fingers.

"So," Celia says, nudging my shoulder, as Jess moves to show the dress to the others. "How's the skin care going?"

I'm wearing a long-sleeved turtleneck with skinny jeans and high socks. The only skin showing is my hands and what's above my neck. She can't see that I've done absolutely nothing with those bottles. Why mess with perfection? "Oh, it's going well! Yeah, just getting smooth and buttery!"

Celia blinks. "Oh, well, that's good! Do you want to show me?"

"No, I think I'm going to save it for the wedding! Besides, I don't want to jinx it."

She glances at my chewed fingernails. "Yeah, but—"

I turn back to the dresses, grab one in my size, and head over to Jess. "Dress looks great! Gonna go check out; got a work thing I forgot about. See you at the next planning meeting!"

"Hey, we're not done yet! And you need to try that on!" my sister calls as I walk away.

"Already did!" I yell back.

That night, I wear my pus dress while masturbating to Amy's vide another time. It fits perfectly.

***

When Celia told us that the cabin was a "cozy, remote, Insta-worthy getaway!", I thought she meant a rustic log cabin at the edge of town. I was not expecting a modern monstrosity twenty miles from the nearest house. It's huge, but somehow all eight members of the "Bride Tribe" are sleeping in bunk beds and sharing a bathroom. All for the low *low* price of $200 per night per person. As the bride, Jess gets the only private room with an en suite and an actual bed.

"Isn't this gorgeous!" she yells, emerging from her room. She gestures out a window to the snowy hills that surround us. "Let's make sure to take lots of great pics! And don't forget to tag them with #JessSaidYes!"

I roll my eyes as we make our way downstairs.

"Hey, what time is Amelia supposed to arrive?" Celia asks.

"She should be here any minute," my sister replies.

"I'm so glad she's able to come to your Bachelorette!" one of the other girls adds. "I was super bummed that she couldn't make it to any of the planning meetings."

"I know! I almost kicked her out of the wedding party for that, but decided to let her pay for my portion of this weekend instead."

"So generous of you!" Celia is quick to say.

I hold in my snort as we all take seats in the large living room. Somehow, the couch manages to look soft while being as comfortable as a rock.

"Okay, so I've got the itinerary here."

Celia passes a stack of papers around our circle. The itinerary is *several* pages long. For a *four*-day event. Why did I even agree to come?

"Tonight we're going to—"

Just then, the front door flies open and a girl steps inside. "Hey bitches! Who's ready to PARTY!" The others scream with excitement and swarm her. This must be the famous Amelia. Something about her looks familiar, but I can't place where we might've met. Eventually, everyone returns to the couches and Amelia sits next to me. "Hi! I'm Amelia!"

"Hey. Delia."

She has a large zit above her right eye. It doesn't look ready to pop, but when it does, I bet it will be beautiful. "Oh, you're Jess's sister? I've heard so much about you!"

I can't imagine what Jess would've told her. Probably nothing good.

I'm saved from speculating by Celia clapping to

get everyone's attention. Then she resumes going over the plan. There's going to be s'mores, games, snowmobiling, and a lot of drinking. The whole trip sounds exhausting. It's only when Amelia turns to ask Celia a question that I realize where I've seen her.

There's a small scar on her neck. Right where an enlarged pore had been. Amelia is Amy.

***

The rest of the night, I watch her. I can't believe it's Amy. I've gotten off to her video countless times and now she's here with me. Like, *really* here. In the flesh. Just looking at her makes me wet. I want to reach out and touch the scar on her neck and imagine I'm squeezing out ten years of gunk. I want to reach my tongue inside and clean it. I want to—

"Jesus, Delia, quit staring!" my sister hisses.

I startle and turn to her.

"Can you be a little less creepy? God! And what's with the long sleeves? It's, like, super hot in here!" Jess tugs at my shirt and I move away.

"Nothing, sorry." I slip through the sliding door and out onto the porch. She's right; I *am* being creepy. Some time out here, away from Amy, will help me calm down. I lean against the railing and stare out at the yard.

"Beautiful, isn't it?" Behind me—*Amy*. She's followed me out here.

"Um, yes. It's very nice." She stands next to me and I struggle to breathe. What the fuck do I do? Is there some sort of protocol for meeting people you get off to? Oh God, she smells really fucking good. What is that? Cedar? Do *I* smell ok? Did I brush my teeth?

I can't take my own thoughts anymore. I blurt out, "I saw your video!"

"What?" She raises her brow, confused.

"The, uh, the pore one? On YouTube?"

Amy laughs. "Wow! Really?"

"Yeah! I, um, love those kinds of videos."

"I do too! That's why I went to Dr. Reynolds, or SkinKing. Those popping videos are soooo satisfying!"

It's the first time I've smiled at anyone in a long time. It feels nice. "It's crazy to see what comes out, you know? Like I'm always shocked at just how *much* there is."

Amy nods. "Exactly! When Dr. Reynolds showed me how much had been in my pore, I was *shook*! I have no idea how it all fit."

I want to ask her what it was like—the stuff that came out. Would that be weird? But then: "So what's your favorite kind of pop? Do you prefer the ones that come out all at once, or the ones they really have to dig for?" The next twenty minutes goes by in a heady flash. Is this what having a friend feels like?

When it's too cold to remain outside, we head back in. And although Amy joins my sister to discuss wedding stuff, I don't mind. Because every time I catch her eye, she smiles at me. I go to bed happier than I've been in years. And when I watch her video again, knowing what she smells like, what her skin looks like up close, I come harder than I ever have before.

***

The next two days are spent playing asinine wedding centric games, drinking copious amounts of alcohol, and listening to Jess talk endlessly about her nuptials. I only survive by stealing glances at Amy. I make sure I'm subtle, though; I don't want to let Jess know that anything is going on. I don't want her to ruin this tentative friendship.

That night, I drink too much. My face feels flushed and everything has a rosy glow. We're all playing some card game and passing around bottles of wine, but I'm too drunk to understand how it's going. I stand up and sloppily insert myself between Amy and Celia on the couch. "Excuse you!" Celia laughs. I think we're all a little drunk.

"It's okayyy," I slur. "I want to sit with my friend Amy."

Jess snorts.

"No, it's true!" I protest, "We *are* friends!"

"Okay, sure, Delia. You made a friend. Congrats! It only took you, what, twenty-eight years?"

"Chill, Jess!" Amy butts in, wrapping her arm around my shoulders. "We're totally friends, Delia! Any girl who loves popping videos as much as I do is cool with me!" The others gag and look away. "Oh shut up! Lots of people like those videos!" She takes another swig of wine and winks at me. I'm so happy I could die. I spend the rest of the night snuggled up against her.

***

I'm drunk again on night three. This time we're playing Never Have I Ever. Most of the girls say stupid shit, like never have I ever cheated on a boyfriend or let him come on my face. But then it's Amy's turn. She looks me dead in the eyes and says, "Never have I ever had sex with a girl." I return her stare and take a shot. She bites her bottom lip. We're the only ones who drink. That night, I touch myself to thoughts of Amy: her exploring my sores and me emptying hers. It's the fastest I've ever climaxed.

***

Day four arrives. The plan is to snowmobile most of the day, return for an early dinner, pack, go to sleep, and leave early the next morning. I've never liked outdoor activities and Jess knows this, so she's not surprised when I tell her I'm too hungover to participate. And she must be getting tired of me, because she doesn't protest. I spend my time taking a long, hot shower and an even longer nap. The quiet is nice. After I wake up, I lounge on my bunk, relishing being alone.

I miss Amy. I've only known her a few days, but it feels like she gets me. I've always kept to myself. Now, though, I might not have to. I pull out my phone and open her video. Knowing her, what she feels and smells like, makes the clip so much better. Before I can hit play, the front door opens. Someone moves around downstairs.

"Delia? It's Amy! Where are you?"

My heart speeds up. What is she doing back already? I open the door and lean into the hallway. "I'm up here!"

Amy bounds up the stairs towards me. She takes in my flushed face and grins slyly. "What are you doing up here?"

Embarrassed, I sit on my bunk. "Nothing! What are you doing back early? Don't you have snowmobiling to do?"

She sits next to me. "The others are almost done. Besides, I wanted to get you alone." Amy looks down and notices her video on my phone. "And it looks like I was right to. I know you've been thinking of me. And I think we're into the same stuff."

She can't be serious. But what if she is? Tentatively, I reach toward her and take her face in my hands. Amy closes her eyes and leans forward, parting her lips slightly. I gently kiss her

cheek. She laughs. "Oh, you're shy, huh?" I ignore her and continue to kiss around her face. Finally, I come to her zit. I flick my tongue out and circle it. It feels so good. I can already imagine how she'll taste. Salty, but maybe a little sweet, too?

"What are you doing?" she says, but I pay no attention and begin sucking on her sore. I was right; she *is* sweet. "Whoa! Hey!" Amy pushes me off of her. "What the fuck?"

"I thought we were having sex!"

"You were sucking on my *zit*."

I stare at her. Did I misunderstand her? Is this not what she likes? "I thought you said you were into that?"

Amy glares at me, shocked. "When your sister said you were into some weird stuff, I thought she just meant, like . . . *bondage* or something." She giggles. "I mean, Jesus Christ, what *is* that? Like some sort of *pimple* fetish? That's disgusting!"

"B-but you said you love watching those videos! Like I do!"

"Yeah, *watching* zits popped, not having someone fucking suck on mine! Like, what the fuck?" She's laughing so hard she's shaking. "Oh my God, Jess is going to *die* when she hears about this!"

I can see exactly how it'll play out. Amy will tell Jess and everyone else. I'll be shunned for the rest of the weekend. And my sister will tell our parents and the rest of our family. They won't understand. I'll be alone. After thinking I'd finally found someone who understood me, the thought is unbearable.

Amy turns towards the door and I don't even think; I just act. I grab her hair, yanking her head back. "You bitch! Let go of me!" She tries to pull away as I drag her from the door. I let go of her hair with one hand and grasp at her torso. I don't know what I'm doing, but I know I can't let her leave. I won't let her ruin my life.

Amy breaks away from me, kicking my legs out. Suddenly, I'm on the ground and she's straddling me, punching my face. She stops when she hears the snowmobiles outside. "Look's like they're back! I can't wait to tell them all about what a psycho bitch you are!"

I surge toward her neck, as if to kiss her, but instead, I bite. *Hard.* Amy tries to scream, but it comes out strangled. She tugs at my face, but I hold fast, pushing my teeth deep into her flesh. Blood runs down the inside of my throat. Although it doesn't taste as good as pus, I feel my body tighten in response. It feels fucking amazing.

I pull as much of her flesh into my mouth as I can before ripping my head back. A chunk of Amy's torn throat hangs between my lips, leaving her sputtering before collapsing on me. I push her off and sit up. She spasms as blood continues spurting from her throat. Amy lifts her hands and tries to stop the bleeding, but she's already lost too much. Her eyes meet mine and it's clear she's trying to say something, so I lean in close. "Y-y-you b-bit—" I put my finger over her lips and shush her.

Downstairs, the door opens and the girls pour in. They'll be coming up here any minute. I know there's no way I can explain what's happened. No way I can clean any of this up. So I might as well finish it. I tell Amy, "You should've just let me taste you." Then I lean down, take her pimple into my mouth, and begin to suck.

On a hot summer night, something enormous screams down from the sky and pierces into the desert not far from the small town of Farchapel. The stories that trickle back from the crater are strange indeed—those who find it and return claim to be forever changed, transformed into the better, ideal versions of themselves they've always wished to achieve.

THE FLESH INHERENT

PERRY MEESTER

Jamie, recent mysterious visitor in town, is a man on the run, all too eager to escape his current form no matter the cost. Sidney, local drunk, would rather face a hole in the ground than the things he's done. As the two men venture into the desert canyons in search of their better selves, they soon discover that what hides there is much more terrible—and eager to lure them in.

WWW.GHOULISH.RIP

AN EMBARRASSING BUT EDUCATIONAL RECOUNTING OF MY FIRST ACCEPTED SHORT STORY

Max Booth III

JOHNNY KNOXVILLE STARTED his career with magazines paying him to injure himself and then write about the experience. Tasers, stun guns, pepper spray . . . all were used to inflict bodily harm for the sake of entertainment. The success of these articles led to the formation of *Jackass,* which solidified his career as a living crash test dummy. I grew up with the *Jackass* generation and still possess an impenetrable fondness for these boys (yes, I realize they are now all men in their 40s and 50s, but in my head they are still, simply, "the *Jackass* boys").

If you've read my novel, *Touch the Night,* you probably have also guessed a large part of my childhood consisted of performing ridiculous stunts with my friends while one of us filmed it. Thankfully, we couldn't quite figure out how to upload files to YouTube, so they mostly remained on someone's computer hard drive. Are they still on that hard drive? Sometimes this question keeps me up at night. I certainly hope they no longer exist. There's nothing incriminating on these videos—well, no *major* crimes, at least—but they are certainly *embarrassing.*

Nobody wants to watch old videos of themselves behaving like . . . well, like jackasses. I wonder how often Knoxville and the rest of his cast look back at early videos and blush. Maybe they don't. Maybe they're still proud. After all, without these past decisions, they would not be the people they are today. When I look back at the many regrets I have about how I've approached certain aspects of shaping my own writing career, I try to remind myself of the same thing. I feel like I am in a pretty decent place right now, and sometimes I wonder if I would still be here if I hadn't first experienced total humiliation. Would I have still managed to get a screenplay produced into a full-length feature film without facing a ridiculous amount of publishing disasters? Are mistakes always a negative thing, or do they sometimes result in worthwhile consequences?

Which brings me to the purpose of this article: my first ever short story acceptance/publication, which is something that is traditionally viewed as a tremendous achievement, and—at the time—I definitely felt pretty damn proud. However, as you'll soon see, I had plenty of reasons for that feeling to quickly fade.

This issue of *Ghoulish Tales* is a special one, after all. The stories found within are written by authors who had never before published a story—at least, not at the time that their submissions were initially accepted by our magazine. So, what better occasion than to recount my own first ever story acceptance?

Writing this article required me to dig deep into my email history and read the exchanges made between myself and the publisher of my first accepted short story. After reading not only his messages, but also my replies, I could not help but feel incredibly ashamed. I also couldn't stop laughing. Which leads me to suspect there's not only an educational aspect of an article like this, but maybe you'll also find it as entertaining as I do now. I've collected the entire email chain I shared with the publisher of my first accepted short story. When appropriate, I have provided an ongoing commentary to add further context. I am not going to name the publisher here, as he appears to have gotten out of the industry for good, and I'm afraid mentioning his name in full will summon him like some kind of shithead wishmaster.

So, with that said, here we go . . .

From: Max Booth III
To: XXXXXXXXXXXX
Sent: Monday, July 18, 2011 6:12 PM
Subject: Zombie Story Submission

I read on facebook you are accepting one more, and seeing as I couldn't find anywhere else to submit, I am sending it to this email—hope that's okay!

We are exactly one email in and already I am deeply embarrassed. "I read on facebook" is without a doubt one of the worst ways to begin any email—the context doesn't matter. Also, ending a story submission with "hope that's okay!"? Honestly, it's a relief the person who received this email turned out to be a deranged lunatic, otherwise I'd feel even more humiliated than I already am.

Keen observers will notice this email was sent in the summer of 2011, which was nearly fifteen years ago, if you're particularly skilled at math. I turned eighteen years old fourteen days before submitting this story. Two months before that, I received my high school diploma.

Here's the publisher's response, 17 minutes later:

From: XXXXXXXXXXXX
To: Max Booth III
Sent: Monday, July 18, 2011 5:23 PM
Subject: Re: Zombie Story Submission

thanks max. i will be reading it at this very second and will get back to you in an houir or so to say yes or no. if the anser is yes, you can get the signed contract scanned and sent back?

And here we go. My first direct communication from XXXXXXXXXXXX, and we are off to a spectacular start. I feel I speak for the entire writing community when I say the one thing every writer hopes to find in potential publishers is an inability to spell words like "hour" and "answer". And, boy howdy, it sure looked like I'd struck gold!

Okay, let's continue . . .

From: Max Booth III
To: XXXXXXXXXXXX
Sent: Monday, July 18, 2011 6:25 PM
Subject: Re: Zombie Story Submission

Yes, I can do that.
—

From: XXXXXXXXXXXX
To: Max Booth III
Sent: Monday, July 18, 2011 5:28 PM
Subject: Re: Zombie Story Submission

ok, i will let you know. getting a few more in so the best one gets into this antho but i can prob use your story for another if its still fun
thanks!
—

From: Max Booth III
To: XXXXXXXXXXXX
Sent: Monday, July 18, 2011 6:36 PM
Subject: Re: Zombie Story Submission

Cool, sounds good to me. I just saw on FB that you want it to be between 5000 and 7000 words, so that probably disqualifies my story which is just over 4000. Hope you like it anyway!
—

From: XXXXXXXXXXXX
To: Max Booth III
Sent: Monday, July 18, 2011 5:43 PM
Subject: Re: Zombie Story Submission

well i got another one in just now thats in the word count i need. but if you are game, i can still look at your story and use it for the next antho if you want. or this other guy might not like the contract i send and walk away. it happens sometimes, not often though
—

From: Max Booth III
To: XXXXXXXXXXXX
Sent: Monday, July 18, 2011 6:44 PM
Subject: Re: Zombie Story Submission

Yeah, that's definitely cool; considering it for the next anthology sounds plenty good to me.

I can already tell this article was a terrible idea, and I haven't even reached the "acceptance" yet.

Hey, speaking of acceptance, looks like I have a new email! Yay! Let's take a look . . .

From: XXXXXXXXXXX
To: Max Booth III
Sent: Tuesday, July 19, 2011 5:55 AM
Subject: Re: Zombie Story Submission

hi max
Ok, here's the deal. as far as your writing style, I was fine with it. the only thing is that, to me, your story is more like a document by a scientist than a story but it isnt that bad that i would reject it outright. i like it, but not enough to want to give you a book for it. (in other words i dont want to pay for it as i dont LOVE it)

but, many writers could care less about the book and just want to be accepted and published.

if thats you, then let me know and i will still use your story and put it in the antho and send you the contract.

if you say "Hell no, i want compensation" thats fine but then i have to reject this particular story and how you want to send more standard stuff with people talking and fighting ect or anything in between.

i'm fine with whatever you wnt to do.

and thanks again for sending it so quickly. if the answer is yes you want in, i attached the cover art for the antho your story would be in.

cheers

And there it is. My first ever story acceptance.

I've read this email so many times since first receiving it in the summer of 2011. When I first opened it, I was overcome with excitement. I was eighteen years old and had been submitting fiction to markets since I was fourteen. Rejection after rejection after rejection after rejection. Four years of *No thanks*. Four years of thinking I'd never be good enough to be published. Then *bam*. This fuckin' guy comes in, and tells me what every writer dreams of hearing: "i like it, but not enough to want to give you a book for it. (in other words i dont want to pay for it as i dont LOVE it)".

Other emotions I have experienced while rereading that email in later years: rage, frustration, and—especially lately—amusement. I do find it very funny

now; however, there was definitely a time where just mentioning the editor's name would send me shaking with anger.

Also, if you're confused about his "your story is more like a document by a scientist than a story but it isnt that bad that i would reject it outright" line, that can be easily explained. The story—titled "Mad"—was originally written for a high school science assignment. The task involved picking a disease of our choice, researching that disease, and writing a report about it. The task did not mention anything about disguising that report inside a short story about zombies, but I decided it would be more interesting that way. So I picked Creutzfeldt-Jakob disease and went a little nuts with it, and much to my delight received an A from my teacher, which is far more compensation than I ever saw from the eventual publisher.

Which, yes, if you read the acceptance above, you'll know: the compensation being offered on this anthology was *only* a contributor's copy, and he couldn't even be bothered to give me one of those. Surely I wouldn't have agreed to such an outrageously rude offer, right? Well, I mean, obviously I did. Otherwise this wouldn't be an article about my first published short story.

If you thought the acceptance was infuriating, just wait until you read my response.

From: Max Booth III
To: XXXXXXXXXXX
Sent: Tuesday, July 19, 2011 10:28 AM
Subject: Re: Zombie Story Submission

hi there. To be fair, I actually didn't think there would be any compensation except for maybe a free copy of the book—and even if that isn't the case, I am still okay with that as I will just buy a copy myself. so what I am saying is yes, if you want to publish the story in it, I am all for that. At this early point in my writing career, I am more about getting my name everywhere as possible. Thank you, and I look forward to hearing from you!

Jesus fucking Christ, Max. You poor goddamn idiot. Oh my god.

I understand why I emailed this, but I desperately yearn for the ability to reach back in time and punch Past Max in the face.

If you are a new writer and somehow you've stumbled upon this article, please listen to me: never settle for exposure. Back in 2015, I wrote a LitReactor article titled "Exposure is Not Payment: Why You Should Start Respecting Yourself as a Writer". Here's an excerpt from that article, where I basically "subtweeted" the publisher of my first accepted short story:

"I've heard actual 'presses' claim that contributor copies are not an industry standard, which is a hilarious and depressing statement. I've even seen some places refuse to dish out electronic copies. Digital files that don't cost the publisher a fucking dime to send. 'Publishers' come up with these laughable excuses, claiming they're afraid the PDFs might circulate. Basically, they don't even trust their own authors to not upload the anthologies on torrent websites. But the truth is, they're holding these back in the hopes that the authors will purchase a copy on Amazon once the book goes live. Because that's their only real targeted audience. They don't have a fan base. They just have the authors they publish, and the authors' families. If you do not receive a contributor copy for your work, then you are being ripped off, pure and simple. If the book is published in print, then you receive a print copy. If it's eBook only, then you get an eBook. If the book is in print, and you don't receive a print copy or an eBook, then you've been fucked.

"This is a common scam I've noticed among the many micropresses that pop up. Typically, they will start off by exclusively publishing anthologies. These anthologies will not pay anything. The press will accept fifteen to twenty authors for each anthology, all writers who are just starting out, naïve and hungry for any kind of publication. Authors find these open calls and they submit and almost nobody is ever rejected. There won't be a contributor copy given because the publisher knows the author will buy a copy, maybe even a few copies, just so the author can see his/her name in print, and (s)he'll go around showing everybody, bragging. The author's friends and family will want to support the author, so they will also buy copies. There will be no author discount. It will be full price. You publish an anthology with at least fifteen people and charge $14.99 for the book, plus shipping, that's nearly $250, before printing costs. You do a dozen or more anthologies like this a year and you start making a serious income. Especially when it's not just the authors buying it, but also their families."

In that article I was describing an anthology mill, and that's exactly what XXXXXXXXXXXX was doing. Publishing more books than anybody could possibly market with any competency. Not offering any actual

compensation. Relying on the authors and the authors' families as the books' sole customers. He also operated under at least half a dozen different company names, to throw people off his scent. What a racket! And of course I fell for it. Not only that, but I was *happy* to fall for it. *This must be what publishing's like*, I foolishly assumed. *Surely nothing shady could be happening here!*

From: XXXXXXXXXXXX
To: Max Booth III
Sent: Tuesday, July 19, 2011 9:58 AM
Subject: Re: Zombie Story Submission

wonderful, glad youre onboard.

and make no mistake, i dont make a habit of doing this. if i had been in a different mood, i might have just sent

you a polite rejection and that would have been it.

will send the contract later.

cheers

It truly baffles me now, reading this all again, just how goddamn *rude* he was in these emails, even after accepting my story. Is this . . . is this what *negging* is? Oh my god, was I *negged*?

Gee, I wonder how I responded this time . . .

From: Max Booth III
To: XXXXXXXXXXXX
Sent: Tuesday, July 19, 2011 11:09 AM
Subject: Re: Zombie Story Submission

Cool, sounds great to me.

And yeah, I figured as much. I am very grateful. Thank you for this.

lmao

From: XXXXXXXXXXXX
To: Max Booth III
Sent: Wednesday, July 20, 2011 6:39 PM
Subject: Re: Zombie Story Submission

hey

havent heard back from you, did you get

the contract? are you scanning and emailing or snail mail?

—

From: Max Booth III
To: XXXXXXXXXXXX
Sent: Wednesday, July 20, 2011 8:00 PM
Subject: Re: Zombie Story Submission

yeah, sorry, I was at a concert last night and have been resting all day from it. I did get the contract. I will print, sign and scan it back to you sometime within the next hour or two.

—

From: XXXXXXXXXXXX
To: Max Booth III
Sent: Wednesday, July 20, 2011 7:22 PM
Subject: Re: Zombie Story Submission

no worries, just checking. see, the story is edited and i want to give it to my proof readers but i dont want them reading something that might not get in if a writer changes their mind. its bad enough i spent the energy editing, i dont want to take up their time too

Thxs

And thus ends the chain of emails chronicling my first short story acceptance. Nearly fifteen years later, the anthology has received one (unrated) review and two ratings on Goodreads. Both ratings are five stars, and they were posted by the same account: an author from the anthology.

This is the only review:

"I have to return this to my to-be-read shelf. I managed to read one story before NaNoWriMo started, 'Justice is Served' (very amusing BTW) and then my mother-in-law absconded with my contributor copy after babysitting for us while my husband and I were at Hal-Con. I don't know when I'll be getting it back, if ever . . . "

What a cliffhanger! Unfortunately I could not figure out if the author's mother-in-law ever returned their contributor copy. Some mysteries are meant never to be solved, I guess.

I wish I could say this also marked the end of all communications with this publisher, and that I never submitted to one of his anthologies again, but of course that isn't true. C'mon. You've read the article this far. You already knew it wouldn't end so easily.

On October 17, 2011, I received the following email (which CC'd 41 authors in total):

Subject: new author's horror antho open

To all XXX and XXX writers,

As writers, there are times we get an idea for a story and then after it's written, we don't know what to do with or can't find a home for it. But dammit, the story is good and you want it to see print so others can read it too.

like in the Book of XXXXXX anthos already made by XXX, XXXX XXXXXX XXXXX (an XXX imprint) is doing the same thing. So if you have a horror story (any type) that's fun and you want to see it in print, send it to me by way of XXXXXXXXXXXX. Editing is still in effect so just 'cause you send it doesn't mean it's in but hopefully it will be. there is no payment for this antho, like in Book of XXXXXX, and the reason is this is my way of helping you get your work out there. these books don't sell alot but I don't care. This one is made for the writers.

Hope you either have something in you library or want to write that story that's been on you mind.

Three days later I submitted a new short story to the anthology. This was also the same month I moved into my first studio apartment after hopping on a bus from Indiana to Texas. I left my entire family behind and began living in a strange state, alone. It was on one of these nights shortly after submitting my new short story that I received a phone call from an unfamiliar number.

You know how when you submit a story, you include your telephone number at the top left of your manuscript, because it's standard practice but you don't actually expect anybody to . . . ya know, *dial it?*

So yeah. Guess who was calling me.

What followed was one of the strangest phone conversations of my life. It lasted at least an hour, if not longer. The man on the phone—who, again, I will not name here—talked with the same speed as a machinegun firing infinite bursts. His voice was only interrupted by brief snorting noises. I don't know for a fact that this man was drowning in cocaine but this man was definitely drowning in cocaine.

The phone call started with him addressing the recent short story I had submitted to his new anthology. He informed me that while he liked it, there was no way in hell he could ever accept it under its current narrative structure. Evidently, stories written in first-person POV were too amateurish for his fine company, and if I wanted to rewrite it in third-person then *maybe* he'd reconsider. He told me no publisher in their right mind would ever accept a story told in first-person POV. This then quickly transgressed into a paranoid rant about how other publishers and authors were "out to get" him and wanted to see him fail. I did not get much room to speak on my end, as he literally never stopped speaking, but I think I managed to fit a couple "Oh, okay"s in. Eventually, the phone call ended, and I went to sleep.

Fast forward about half a year later, and an another author writes a blog post that pretty much destroys what little career this publisher might have managed to make for himself. I won't link to the writer's blog post here, as it was over a decade ago and there's no reason to reopen old wounds, but *holy crap*. In this particular case, XXXXXXXXXXXX not only added a typo to the author's story, but he also added *an implied rape scene,* along with other details seemingly from the editor's imagination; things that did not exist in the story until after the author sent it to the publisher. And of course XXXXXXXXXXXX did not send edits for approval before publishing. He released it and the author only discovered what had happened to their story after flipping the paperback open, which I'm sure they had to purchase themself. The author emailed XXXXXXXXXXXX about the situation, and if you've read the previous emails copy/pasted in this article, then you can probably guess he responded like a true dickhead. So the author wrote up a blog post

documenting everything that had happened, and it blew up, with people like Neil Gaiman even sharing it (I originally wrote a version of this article long before the Gaiman allegations came to light, but I'm choosing to keep the reference here because it's true he did call out the publisher, but also it sure is depressing how often the most vocal people about this sort of gross shit turn out to also be a much worse kind of monster). Nowadays, nobody mentions this dude's name, and for good reason. I don't think he's still publishing, at least not under any obvious names.

This article was not written to *expose* anybody, as he's already been exposed and rightfully exiled from the horror community. Instead I wanted to share the story of my first accepted short story, and I've done that. I hope you found it amusing. I also hope, if you are a new writer, you can take my past experiences as some sort of lesson. There are lots of grifters out there looking to take advantage of naive authors. It's not always easy to see the signs, especially when nobody else has written about getting duped. So consider this article a cautionary tale. If a publisher accepts your story while simultaneously insulting you, maybe just tell them to go fuck themselves. Also, don't submit to markets not offering fair compensation. Have pride in your work. Do not settle because you have a desperate desire to see your name in print. It's not worth it. It's never worth it.

And now, to close out this issue of stories written by never-before published authors, I thought it might be fun—or, at the very least, *interesting*—to leave you with the story referenced in this article. The one I wrote for science class back when I was seventeen, that would eventually get published (for free) in a terrible zombie anthology a year later. It's never going to be included anywhere else at this point, so I thought it might be a good idea to bury it once and for all in the back-end of *Ghoulish Tales: New Ghouls Edition*. A final resting place that isn't stigmatized with shame.

So, uh, here it is, in all its unedited glory. Enjoy?

MAD

Max Booth III

THIS WILL BE A report on the Creutzfeldt-Jakob disease (CJD) epidemic that has penetrated the unincorporated community of Jonesville, Butte County, California; population 425,000. The date is May 31st, 2016. My name is Brian Fitzgerald, head researcher for the CDC team recruited to investigate the Jonesville Prion Contamination; and as of this writing, I have no idea who is infected and who isn't. I do not know who is still alive, or who is dead. As a matter of fact, I am not even certain if I will still be sane by this time tomorrow—or, for that matter, in a couple hours. I just don't know.

I will begin this report by apologizing for not checking in sooner. I realize that our first priority was designing a plan of action for the city council, but by the time I am finished relaying the following events, you will understand that this has proven to be more difficult than any of us could have ever thought possible. At this moment, I am barricaded in my hotel room; a dresser has been pushed against the door, although I do not know how long this will last. Fortunately the room is on the third floor, otherwise I would have had to do the same for the window. I am sitting behind a large Mahogany desk; present in front of me is a uniform gooseneck lamp, a bottle of Jack Daniels three quarters of the way empty, the word processor which I am currently typing this report on, and a Beretta M9. The pistol's magazine is currently housing thirteen out of fifteen possible bullets. I would be lying if I said I was not aware of the use of those two missing bullets; a man—a man of science, no less—was killed this morning by my own hand. I fired two shots off; one in his chest, the other in his head. I am not proud of this,

but my job is to report to you every fact and this, I feel, is a pretty important fact.

The facts are this: three months ago a CJD report was sent in by a local Jonesville mortician. While this in itself is a very rare incident, the Centers for Disease Control did not act right away as we should have. However, three weeks ago, we received another report by the same mortician—who, understandably enough, was quite concerned—of another case of Creutzfeldt-Jakob disease. Another unusual detail in these cases was the victims' ages, both of whom were in their early 20s—whereas most of those who suffer from CJD are in their 60s and up. Discovering the extremely young ages of both cases and how close together the deaths had been, the CDC was given enough reason to issue an investigative team out on the site.

I was leader of that investigation. As of now, I cannot account for the whereabouts of most of my team. I know some of them are dead; others, I can only pray, have escaped from the area.

Given the young ages of the two victims, we were able to determine that the form of disease was, in fact, new variant CJD (vCJD); a type of Creutzfeldt-Jakob disease that affects people considerably below the average age of those who suffer from CJD. This diagnosis quickly became the concern for our entire team, as all indications pointed toward the consumption of a possible beef contamination—and, as until now, there had only been one case of vCJD being contacted this way in the United States; in the whole world, there has been over 150 people infected by contaminated beef, all of whom primarily live in the UK.

In new variant CJD, the disease can be spread through exposure to brain or nervous system tissue (usually through medical procedures)—or, in other cases, by contaminated beef. It has been unknown whether or not one can become infected with CJD through blood or plasma; previous studies on animals have suggested contaminated blood may transmit the disease, although this has not been ascertained with humans—up until now.

Here, barricaded in my hotel room, the screams of the crazed continue pouring in from outside, I can state without a doubt in my mind that the disease can indeed be transmitted by blood. I have witnessed its ability from first-hand experience, along with witnessing many other things that I wish could be erased from memory. I have seen what this disease can do. The pistol on my desk is enough proof of that.

When we arrived in Jonesville, we did not fear for our own safety. There was no reason to: this disease does not travel airborne, nor through water and casual contact. In fact, the one person most in danger of becoming infected with such a disease would have been the mortician himself from having performed the autopsy of two such victims, although we did not anticipate such an unlikely reaction at the time. We did not anticipate much of anything that would follow. How could we?

Considering that both victims had contracted vCJD, we could not simply rely on coincidence as an explanation. Therefore, I issued a portion of my team to purchase a few pounds of beef from the local supermarkets, and to test it for any nefarious activity. Sure enough, the next day they returned to me and reported that they had bought a pound of meat from each market within a five miles radius, and every one of them had tested positive for bovine spongiform encephalopathy—or, as it is better known, mad cow disease. As its nickname explains rather bluntly, BSE is a disease that only affects cattle; symptoms would include obnoxious drooling, unreasonable fear, grinding of teeth, consistent staggering, and unusual aggression toward fellow animals. It makes them quite literally mad.

Now, if a human were to ingest the meat of a cow riddled with BSE, then that human would become infected as well; only when we are talking about humans, the disease is instead now called vCJD, as previously mentioned. The symptoms are pretty similar to mad cow disease, only a lot more powerful: the victim suffers from a rapidly progressive form of dementia; uncontrollable crying and/or screaming; severe personality changes such as impaired memory, judgment, thinking and vision; insomnia; depression; occasional blindness; and all around a series of strange sensations. Initially, the infected individual might experience problems with muscle coordination, and as time passes, it will progress into strong muscle jerks called myoclonus; eventually, they will lose the ability to move and speak altogether and end up in a coma. It

is true that some of these symptoms are quite identical to other neurological disorders like Alzheimer's and Huntington's disease, but CJD differs with unique brain tissue changes seen at the autopsy and by more rapid deterioration of a person's abilities than these other diseases. Like the cows, the humans will be turned completely mad.

Once receiving the BSE test results, I immediately contacted every market within the city and ordered them to pull all stocks of beef from their shelves. Of course, most of them did not want to oblige willingly, but after some empty threats and questionable declarations, I was finally able to convince them all that I was in fact being serious: all of the beef in the city would be considered contaminated until further tests could be carried out. I understood how this would affect profits, but I was left with little choice.

Afterward, I gave my team instructions to collect more product from the grocery stores and follow through with more testing. While they did this, I (and a few others in my group) headed back to the city morgue, where we commenced to studying the two vCJD victims—whom had already been isolated in their own little room thanks to the mortician.

Now, the mortician was an odd man; he would begin to join us in analyzing the situation, only to abruptly change the conversation around to his mother, whom was now dead, but he assured us many times that she had been an excellent cook. Then he would continue to talk about the two cadavers until stopping mid-sentence, having forgotten what he was going to say. At the time, we all figured he had just been an old man in need of an early retirement. On retrospect, however, I had been a fool not to notice the signs. They were so obvious, and I had failed to see them. Although, even if I had realized what was wrong with the mortician, there was nothing I could have done to save him; he was already dying—as was everyone else in the city. We may have stopped the sale of beef, but we'd arrived too late; they never had a chance.

There was no saving them.

Back at the morgue, my associates and I went to work on the corpses without a moment's waste. Their brains had become almost deformed looking; under the microscope, their brain tissue appeared to be violated with innumerable holes drilled into the cortex, giving it the resemblance of a sponge. It was the trademark feature of transmissible spongiform encephalopathy—otherwise known as prion disease. I had already anticipated this discovery; although never seeing a brain like this firsthand, I had certainly read my share of information about the matter.

The prion, an infectious protein, is unlike any other

bacteria or virus known to man; while normal infectious agents require some kind of nucleic acid to exist (DNA, RNA, or both), the prion protein does not contain any such gene. Transmissible spongiform encephalopathy, the diseases caused by these prions (which both of the victims had suffered from) can be associated with four characteristics: spongiform change, neuronal loss, astrocytosis, and amyloid plaque.

There are two kinds of the prion protein (PrP): properly-folded (PrP-C; meaning common or cellular) and disease-linked and misfolded (PrP-SC; named after scrapie, the first known prion disease). The PrP-SC enters a healthy organism and right away makes itself at home; meaning, the prion will begin to convert normal PrP-C into a diseased state; these newly adapted proteins will then go on to convert more and more protein, which only proceed to do the very same thing, triggering a chain reaction that produces an immense volume of the abnormal prion form. This mass of misfolded proteins interrupts all cell function and subsequently causes cell death; alterations in conformation puts an end to the protein's ability to undergo digestion. It is all maintained by invading the brain and producing itself in one surreal, self-sustaining feedback loop.

Such structural stability means these prions are incredibly resistant to heat, chemicals, and even radiation. They cannot be inactivated with disinfection measures used to destroy other disease-causing agents. There is, in fact, no way of stopping them. There is no cure. There is no anything. Once they're in, there is no getting them back out.

The next morning, I began to make rounds at doctor offices inquiring over any unusual patients. I was quite mortified to discover that there had been more than just a few recent diagnoses of borderline dementia, as well as more patients who were suffering from some of the other very same symptoms that those with CJD suffer from. I collected a handful of these patients and brought them back to the hospital, where I put them on top priority for treatment.

We gave them the whole nine yards: spinal taps to rule out other more common cases of dementia; electroencephalograms to record brain patterns; computerized tomography of the brain to help rule out the probability that the symptoms were the result from a stroke or brain tumor; and MRIs, which can often reveal characteristic patterns of brain degeneration that can help diagnose CJD. All of these results started to lean toward an outcome I did not want to think about; but nothing was for sure. At least not then. The only way to truly confirm a case of CJD is either by a brain biopsy or an autopsy—and, since these patients were still alive, we decided to go with the former.

I already knew what the biopsies would say before we even did it. I had had this feeling in my gut that whole morning; a feeling like there was a storm coming, and everything would drown in its wake. It was a sensation I had been experiencing since first arriving in the city. Nothing good would come from my stay here, and the biopsy results proved just that.

Of course, I was right: the results came back positive for vCJD—and, sure enough, when we took another biopsy of another patient the following week, these results reported positive as well. By then, we had already set up roadblocks around the area. We didn't know how many people in the city were infected, and there was no way to tell; it wasn't like we could go around giving door-to-door brain biopsies. No one knows how all the city's beef products became infected like it did, but it doesn't mean this is only happening here; other shipments of meat could also be contaminated, and they are being consumed right now as I type this. I urge you to order mandatory BSE tests for all of the United States. This is nothing else I can do about the matter except finish this report. I don't even have a phone to call for help now. I just have this word processor that lacks an Internet connection. Truthfully, I have not thought about how I am going to send this report out until now, but I am sure one of your men will come across it—I just hope that it is not too late by the time you do.

I'm pretty sure I'm infected, by the way. I don't know if I made that clear. I haven't been feeling very good all day. I've been careful, too. I've defended myself well; no blood has gotten on me, no brain tissue, no gore, no anything. My best guess would be back when I first arrived here, and was experimenting with the brains of the first two cadavers. Perhaps I had been neglectful. I do not know. It doesn't really matter now, I suppose. I'm finding it harder to make my fingers type the keys I want to type. I am growing tired of typing. Typing. It. Tried of grow typing. I am going 2 eyes for a rest 4 a few soon

It's around 5 in the evening now. I dozed off for a while. It didn't help; the situation is still the same. There is no sleeping and waking up to a better tomorrow. The prion is still alive, still in me, still in us all. If I look out my window, I can see the occasional pedestrian running wildly down the street. On the curb, next to a streetlamp, there is a puddle of blood; it's so dark and thick looking. You can see crimson footsteps leading away from the puddle, disappearing behind a family restaurant. I dined at that restaurant a few times during the three weeks I've been stationed here. I made sure not to order anything with beef. Like that's really helped, right?

I don't remember ever reading a CJD case where the victim lashed out with violence before. Something is different with this case. I regret to admit I do not know what that is. There was simply not enough time for proper testing. The normal incubation period for CJD should be years—in most cases, even decades—yet, with this mutated version of vCJD, people begin showing symptoms in as little as hours after being infected. Some last longer, some last even shorter. It just doesn't make any sense.

And as I have previously mentioned, this disease can indeed be transmitted through blood. I am able to determine this from an incident three days ago, when this whole situation really began to spin out of control. I was leaving the hospital with a few other members of my team. We boarded the elevator and discovered the mortician leaning against the floor buttons. He was just standing there, staring at his feet, and sobbing silently. There was a line of blood streaming from out of the corner of his lips—I can only assume he had been chewing on his own tongue. We tried calling his name but he did not respond. Then one of my associates laid a hand on his shoulder, and the mortician snapped out of his daze at once. He looked up at my associate with a pair of these miserable foggy eyes, and before any of us knew what was wrong, the mortician opened his mouth and ripped a good chunk of flesh from my associate's neck. There was much screaming then, and lots of blood; so much blood. The mortician was crazy. He started lashing out at us all. Blood squirted from my associate's neck. (Perhaps some of it got in my mouth or my eyes; that would also be a perfectly reasonable explanation for my probable infection.) It took quite a struggle, but we were finally able to subdue the mortician: we knocked him out by repeatedly banging his skull against the elevator door—barbaric, yes, but also very effective. We got the attention of the authorities and they chained the mortician to a bedpost up in one of the hospital rooms. My associate was also admitted to a room, although his injury was not as damaging as it had appeared in the elevator; all it took was a few stitches, and he was fine. He was able to check himself out that very night.

Unfortunately, I would not be given the chance to examine the mortician any further than I was able to in the elevator, for things only began to escalate from there. Apparently, a large sum of the city's population was infected, just like I had feared—and, for some reason, they all began to show symptoms almost simultaneously. Unlike other CJD cases, they were all associated with an abnormal rage; almost as if this new prion form destroys serotonins as well, turning them into these crazed killing machines.

Since then, the streets have not been safe to walk. The infected are everywhere, it seems. I've watched survivors stumbling around outside confused, only to be attacked moments later by a drooling lunatic. I tried to warn them from my window but it only distracted long enough for one of the infected to sneak up on them. God knows how the roadblocks are handling all of this. Have they broken free of the city? Have they migrated toward other populations? I don't know. Is this just an isolated event, or is this happening in other places besides Jonesville? What the hell has happened?

This is not coincidental. Something disrupted the city's beef supply with BSE-infected cattle carcasses. We are talking hundreds upon hundreds of pounds of beef—all contaminated. Such a disaster should have been impossible; and yet, it has happened, and the results are miles beyond the normal definition of terror. I am left with the only conclusion that outside parties must be responsible; perhaps a foreign group of terrorists who had the access and the ability to infiltrate the country's beef supply—a group that, somehow, have managed to escape our radars. Such an attack would have taken years of formation, and precise action to carry it out successfully; and somehow, they have. If this is only the beginning, God only knows what else they have in store for us. The possibilities are cataclysmic.

I became separated from most of my team just last night, when a large group of infected burst into the hospital and began attacking everyone. We had been all gathered around in the cafeteria feasting over our supper when the crazies came storming through the doors, lunging anyone within reach. I witnessed from my table as one of my associates had a large pipe driven through her face, while another one was bashed in the skull with a brick; others were bitten, clawed, torn apart, and all around dismembered. Many, though, were able to flee the scene. I do not know where they are now; I can only hope they are safe.

The infected jumped at me as well, but I managed to defend myself without being injured. I can very vividly recall one gentleman was able to tackle me to the ground; despite holding the man's hands back while he wrestled on top of me, he still tried to snap at me with his teeth. Long thin lines of blood were dripping from his mouth, and if I had not thrown him off of me in time then it would have undoubtedly spilled into my own opened mouth. There was a broken chair leg nearby that I swung at the rest of the attackers as I fled from the building, along with the only other survivor in the room: my associate whom had previously been bitten by the conformed mortician. We managed to board ourselves up in my hotel room, having first confiscated the aforementioned Beretta M9 from a dead policeman's holster. I don't think either one of us slept much all night. We haven't really said much to each other either. What is there to say? There is nothing. We just stayed up here listening to the screaming and the crying and the killing. It is madness.

Then in the morning I woke up, having finally nodded off at sunrise, and discovered my associate kneeled down in front of me, just watching me like I was some mysterious creature. For a moment I feared the worst: that I had turned into one of the crazies roaming around outside, that I had become one of them, one of those monsters. However, it did not take long to realize that the monster wasn't me, it was him. His arms were jerking, his teeth chattering frantically; I looked him in the eyes and asked if he was okay. He did not hear me. A single tear dripped down his check, and then he screamed into my face and backhanded me across the jaw as hard as he could. I flew to the ground, my mouth bleeding, and fumbled for the pistol in my jacket pocket. I knew what needed to be done and did not intend on wasting any time. He started to charge toward me screaming madly, and I raised the gun; two deafening bangs later and I was the only living soul left in the hotel room. Now it all smells so rancid, I can't bear it anymore. I'm sitting here at my desk looking at the corpse across the room and it all makes me want to vomit but if I do that it will just make it smell worse and I just want to leave this place already I want to go back to my home

where no one is killing anyone no one is infected it is my home this is a strange land I do not know these people these people are going to kill me they have killed me look at the gun on the desk it will kill me like it's killed my associate whom I don't even know the name of

who all are dead I do not know, they are all dead maybe, maybe they are dead yes, maybe. Still no one understands I do not understand what has happened here in this place this strange land I do not know this place I do not these things

I do not

I can't stand this much longer I swear TO GOD I DON'T want this I can't do it there's so much sweat I keep sweating I don't know why I don't know why anything and no one does
why would they

they are just infected too. THEY are all infected we are and you are and I am and he is and she is and the world is and everyone is

infected

There's no more whiskey left in my bottle I think I might go look and find some more and maybe I will find a way a key with cars in it and leave this place for good and everything will be okay I can see my family they are waiting for me
the thing is
                    i dont know what the thing is

its too hard to type now i think i am going to i dont remember my mOTHERS name what is her
naMe i want to talk to her where is she why are this here PINK dress she pink with flowers I remember she is now and I am too
there are more outside
my gun is empty there are no bullets nO whiskey no anyTHing
where is it all

?

i wonder what the mortician is doing

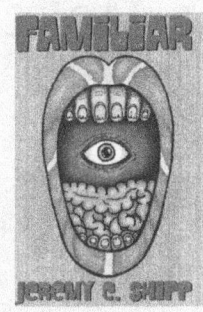
Live Spooky, Die Spooky.

Would really
you
want
your
book to
look
like
this?

No, of course not!

You've worked hard to complete your
masterpiece.
Make it look as professional as you are.

www.TheAuthorsAlley.com

ABOUT OUR GHOULS

Madelyn Lunnen doesn't give a shit about author bios.

Melissa Nowark is a microbiologist, serial hobbyist, and cat parent. When not bed rotting, they love traveling to a new bookstore or stationery shop. They are passionate about human rights, mental health, and chronic illness advocacy. They currently live in South Carolina with their partner and five cats.

Harrison Stypula is a writer of weird, queer horror and a lover of good tea. They have read for both *The Skull and Laurel magazine* and Cat Eye Press. They have a BA in English from Seton Hill University, and live in Greensburg PA with their partner.

Miguel Villa is a failed podcast host trying his luck at writing horror comics and short stories. He likes horror movies and Ice Nine Kills.

M.E. Wilczek is a former ethical hacker who still hacks some of the time and is ethical most of the time. She lives in Concord, MA with her husband, her son, and two dogs.

M.M. Williams is an author of Norse-inspired Fantasy novels and spooky short fiction. A native of the Pacific Northwest, she currently roams the wilds of Northern Utah with her spouse, toddler, and tyrannical tortoiseshell cat. She'll soon have stories in the *Loki* and *Werewolf* anthologies by Flame Tree Press.

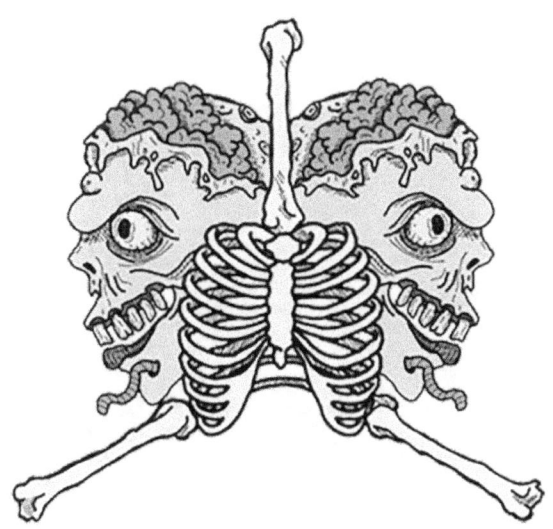

www.ingramcontent.com/pod-product-compliance
Lightning Source LLC
Chambersburg PA
CBHW080842250626
47161CB00009B/3155